VIC HOLYFIELD AND THE CLASS OF 1957

Cover designed by Bill Toth

Book design by Iris Bass

Cover art courtesy of Risa Kessler

Author photograph by Layle Silbert

VIC HOLYFIELD AND THE CLASS OF 1957

a romance

William Heyen

AVAILABLE
PRESS

BALLANTINE BOOKS • NEW YORK

1

It's hard to get started, but the nights are long here, so I've got plenty of time.

Eddie Rogas and I have the night shift. When we're not walking the halls or patrolling outside between the building and the fence, we sit at desks on the ground floor. He's on the north side, by that entrance. I'm sitting over by the south entrance.

A little while ago, checking the grounds, I smelled lilac and honeysuckle in the night air from bushes that are growing by the main doors, near the flagpole. I smelled those same blossoms when I was a kid and went to school here. But I didn't pay attention then. I'd just swing off the bus and breeze into school. But something in me must have registered those smells, and remembered. Now, here I am again, and thirty-odd years have gone by on my old Long Island, and the same lilac and honeysuckle bushes scent the air, and I don't know for sure if I'm any wiser than that kid I was. I hope I am, but how can I be sure? Even after last year, I don't know.

But never mind me, except to say that of all of us in Vic's class I'm the one to tell the story, and all my classmates know it, or should know it. I don't know what Vic would think about my writing all this down. I'll keep it to myself, for now. If Eddie in his loneliness walks over this way, it will look like I'm writing a letter. No, I do know: Vic wouldn't mind. He knows me better than anyone else does except maybe Ellen. He'd know what is underneath what's being said.

Moonlight is shining in from a hall window behind me, and
the light from my desk lamp makes a small moon on this sheet
of paper. It's hard to get started.

Music from upstairs where Vic lives. He's in the Ballad
Room, listening to Dion singing "No One Knows." Eddie and I
can hear it softly but clearly down here. The music connects me
with Vic, as it always has. The slow and sad song gets me to
dreaming and remembering again. . . . I don't think Vic will
ever leave here, at least not for long.

2

I'd seen the auction announcement in the local papers—this was
early summer a couple years ago. Smithtown High School was
closing for good, at least the old building on New York Avenue
was, and the school district was selling the three-story brick
building and all its contents. Desks and maps and file cabinets
and books and framed pictures of Lincoln and Washington and
drapes from the auditorium and such stuff would begin selling
on a Saturday morning a few weeks later. That same afternoon
"at one o'clock sharp," as the ad said, the building itself would
be sold "without reserve to the highest bidder." There was a
minimum bid of fifty thousand dollars. The property alone
would be worth fifty grand, I guessed, but what would anyone
want with the place? Maybe it would be turned into apartments,
as had many such schools across this now zero-population-
growth America. Maybe it would be demolished.

When I saw the ad I thought of my old high school behind

the maples. I'd only walked past it once or twice since I'd been back in Smithtown. I didn't think it would bother me that it would be emptied out and maybe renovated or leveled. But I found myself thinking hard about it from the minute I saw the auction ad. In fact, I was thrown by the ad. The thing is that at that time it was as though my life was moving faster on me than I could understand it or locate myself, and the announced auction of the school didn't help focus or slow things down for me.

There, in that square red-brick building, four years of my life stood still in time, and were there and always would be there for me to think about and understand when I'd someday maybe have the time to do some serious thinking. Years before, someone had published a book called something like *Is There Life After High School?* I only heard about it, but knew what it had to be about.

For years I'd listened once in a while to my "oldies but goodies." The feelings that filled me as I listened—well, these were the same feelings that grew in me as I thought about my old high school building. I've had a life after high school, maybe too much of the wrong kind of life most times, but a life. Our earth has sailed through the universe since I graduated in 1957—I understand that our whole solar system is heading in the general direction of the constellation Virgo—but the light in that old building, its sounds and smells, its lives, exist in some dimension that Vic knows better than the psychologist who wrote that book.

3

Almost anyone who happened to read that his or her old high school building was going on the auction block would be *interested,* at least, to use a neutral word. I wanted to go to the auction. I cut out the ad and slapped a magnet over it on my refrigerator door, as though I would need a reminder.

I began to think of what I could buy. Maybe a desk with a date from the 50s carved into it. Maybe one of the trophies from the hall cases. Maybe *the* trophy from our league basketball championship. Yes, if it was there, I'd try to buy the trophy. Who else would want it? Two new high schools, Smithtown East and Smithtown West, had been built, and the kids had enough of their own trophies by now. I wanted mine, ours, if it was going to be sold. But I was just blabbering to myself, feeling edgy and displaced because my old school was shaking on its foundations somewhere deep inside me where it had stood so solid, deep as the smells of honeysuckle and lilac, for decades. I was just being paranoid. No doubt the trophy was in a case in one of the new schools.

Vic is restless. He's moved over to the Fast Dance Room. Little Richard is screeching to Miss Molly. I remember when Vic and Eddie and Andy Caruso and my brother Werner and I drove to the New York Paramount for a live show of about twenty groups over Christmas vacation in 1958. Right after the Alan Freed movie, the curtains closed and then Little Richard walked through them, cape of green sequins, pink shirt,

high-piled hair, silver stilt shoes. He yelled "Do you want it?"
Yeah, the audience yelled. "Do you want it?" he yelled again.
Yeah, we all yelled louder. Firecrackers were coming down
out of the balconies, cops were beating on the kids that began to
dance in the aisles. "Do you want it?"

Little Richard has lost the faith and got religion. He says he's
traded rock for the Rock of Ages, roll for the Roll of Glory in
the sky. I still like the man, but sometimes I think that Elvis is
better off.

4

It was at the auction that I first saw Vic again. There was a
knot of people around someone out in front of the auctioneer's
platform. It never crossed my mind that Vic would be there
until I saw that group of people staying close to someone. It's
not that they were with him or even talking to him. It's just
that there was someone at the center of a group bigger and
more intense than the scattered threes and fives across the lawn.
When I saw a flashbulb go off over there, one went off in my
head and I thought of Vic. Yes, there was a reporter and a
photographer, and my old friend was there. I got closer, stood
about twenty feet behind him. I could see he was annoyed by
the press.

He looked good. That's about all I could think of when I saw
him. I'd seen pictures of him since high school, but figured I
couldn't really tell how he was doing from the pictures, or from
the stories either for that matter. But here he was, tanned, in

good shape, only slightly overweight, if at all. His black hair had some gray in it now and had thinned a little, but he still combed it straight back in a modified d.a. He was wearing a rumpled blue suit worn at the elbows. He was no doubt usually on the run and too busy to worry about his clothes. He wasn't here, either, to impress the hometown folks. He had his hands in his pockets, his jacket collar was turned up, he looked a little seedy, but it was Vic.

Well, yes, the press would be where Vic was, but why was he here? I suppose I'd been jealous in some way of his success, though that success was so overwhelming that I wasn't much more jealous than I could have been about someone winning a billion-dollar lottery.

I'd always cared for Vic, but had my own versions of him, and skimmed rather than read the stories about him, even the *Newsweek* cover story about ten years ago. A few times, I almost called him, but didn't, and was glad in the end that I didn't. I wondered if he needed me, maybe, as I always felt Elvis needed one true friend, one friend with some brains who could talk to him about the ways in which he would have to deal with the phenomenon he was, the ways he would have to mature. One friend. I tried—that's all I'll say.

I kept my life to myself, and Vic became one of the world's two or three richest men.

He lived in Texas. At least his home base was there. What I'd gleaned as I paid half-attention to the stories sounded like a character sketch for a romance novel: electronics, dozens of computer patents for him after he left graduate school at Cornell with three degrees in four years; franchises ("Vic's Shacks") pouring monies in to him; then, all of that strange wheeling and dealing in the silver market—he actually at one time owned about ninety percent of the world's silver. Then, apparently, arms sales, the outfitting of whole armies in Africa and South America. That was his "cynical period," he told me a month ago. He says he's gotten out of that. Too many bad dreams, he says.

I'd been contacted about him several times, reporters going through the high school yearbook and hitting on his classmates. I never said anything except "You'd better ask Vic about that."

Vic at the auction of his old high school. People beginning to come up to him, introducing or reintroducing themselves. I saw some ghosts myself. Dr. Bowes, our principal, long retired, now chatting at Vic, his wife fluttering as though Vic were royalty. Vic distracted, looking through them.

I wanted him to come to *me,* but knew he wouldn't.

But then he did. First he glanced around behind him, and we looked into each other's eyes. He looked away quickly. Then—I'm six foot five—he knew. He looked into my eyes again, moved through some people. We walked to each other. We gave each other one of those embarrassed male jock back-slapping hugs. I felt everybody else at the auction watching us.

There was some small talk. I can't/don't want to remember my part in it. I've always been shy, and habitually look at the ground when I speak to people. Fact is, face to face I couldn't tell you this whole story that I'm telling.

Vic kept his right hand on my left shoulder. We faced the auction platform, looking straight ahead while talking to each other. People didn't bother us, probably because he had his hand on my shoulder, making us our own private center. Only one of our old teammates could have joined us, but I hadn't seen any.

"I've missed you, Billy," he said. "I wanted to call you, get in touch with you, send for you—I mean ask you to visit. Especially these past few years. I've wanted to come to the Island to see you. But I wanted to leave you alone, too, you know? I knew you wouldn't be in touch with me first. I know you."

He talked, and I listened. This was the way it had been in high school, and will probably always be. But I was not a "sapper," he once told me, someone who drains the energy of other more creative people and leaves them exhausted. He once said I was a "creative listener." That's board-room jargon, but

he was right. I've never missed much. It takes some hard
listening to know what's really being said.

I looked down at the ground, or up at the auctioneer's
platform, or glanced left at Vic. I noticed that he was still an
inch or two shorter than me, though I'd somehow thought that
by then he would be taller. Photos usually showed Vic dwarfing
others around him, for one thing. For another, we come to
think the famous are taller than they are.

I began to relax. I could feel my face cool as my blush faded.

I do remember that I asked him one thing: "How long you
here for?"

"I don't know," he said. "We never left," he said.

5

The ten wide marble steps at the school's center entrance were
piled high with desks, lockers, books. The auction platform
looked like a junk shop. The lawn behind the platform looked
like a Salvation Army store after a storm had taken its roof off.
If Vic hadn't been there, I'd have rummaged among the stuff
until, maybe, something connected with me. But I was glad to
be with Vic, and the auction began.

So did the rain, but just a drizzle. We could hear it in the
century-old maples above us. A man in shades came up to
Vic—my first mind flash was that he was a druggie, and this
shows where I still was—and handed him an umbrella. I hadn't
even noticed this bodyguard before, but now saw a couple others
around us too. Vic held the umbrella above us.

A guy by the name of Chet Wilcox was the auctioneer. He
wore a Stetson and string tie, stood in glittery boots at a podium
with his hammer. He made a sappy speech, saying he wasn't
from around these parts himself, podnuh, but that if he had
flunked his way through this school he'd sure want something
to remember it by. He said that even if there were hundreds of
desks, for example, auction bargains were usually there at the
beginning, so we shouldn't wait but should get into the action
early, wave our cards, bid, or we'd lose out. He seemed to be
looking straight at Vic. He said that the building and property
would sell at one sharp, podnuh, and that if any of us in the
crowd wanted to mosey around the building before then and see
his foreman, who had pitched camp in a room on the first floor,
we were welcome to do so. He said it would be a good long
auction, so let's get started.

For about a half-hour Vic just watched as chairs and fire
hoses and bulletin boards and bookshelves were sold. I could
sense that he was nervous, agitated. But sometimes, too, he
seemed distracted and drifted away, all the way to Texas, or
1957, or wherever, or whenever.

When two of the auctioneer's helpers held up a section of
gym lockers, I saw Vic lurch awake and exchange a look with
one of the bodyguards, who held up Vic's number, number 7,
and kept holding it up until he'd bought the battered green
junk. There were good-natured giggles when the crowd realized
who'd bought the lockers. The bodyguard moved forward to
carry the clanking junk away. Another took his place next to
Vic.

I hadn't even signed up for a bidding number. Vic had been
there early, very early. He'd probably asked for number 7.

"Billy, you know, I don't know what the hell I'm doing," Vic
said. "I belong in Kings Park." Kings Park is a mental
institution on the Island.

He bought the marble bust of Homer that had been in the
library since the sack of Troy. He bought the oak library tables.
He let the library books go, except for a huge unabridged

dictionary that had been in the school talking to itself since our time. He bought the lab fixtures from the science room—it took two of his men to lug the marble-basined experiment table away. People weren't giggling now, but were wondering what Vic was up to, the "visiting" between sales becoming louder and louder. Chet had to tell the folks that this was a sale, not a quilting party, and to hush down.

I looked back behind the auction crowd to where Vic's men were carrying all the stuff. There was as much back there now as there was on the platform. "I don't know what the hell I'm doing," Vic said again. Under the umbrella, the rain increasing now, I could smell him, the lime fragrance of his deodorant or aftershave. He's about six months older than I am, but I felt and still feel protective toward him, as though he were the kid brother I never had.

I didn't say anything. I took the umbrella from him and held it above us. I could feel my heart beating. I was afraid.

One of Vic's men brought coffee over to us.

I was afraid. I knew that my life, right then, was changing. Above us, the school building darkened in the rain.

6

At a little after one o'clock that August afternoon in 1987, after futile opposition from a local developer, Vic bought the old Smithtown High School on its four acres for $112,000. He left some of his men behind with instructions to buy the rest of the auction. He told me he had to clear up some things in New

York and then back in Dallas. He said he'd call me in about a week. I said something stupid like "It was good seeing you again, Vic." He looked into my eyes and said, "Billy, I'll be back, you know. This time I'll be back. We have to talk. I've had conversations with you for years. I've known where you were. Maybe you've known I've been in touch with you, and maybe you haven't, but you know what I'm telling you now. And I know I can count on you." As did everyone else, I watched him walk away.

I stayed until the end, watching Vic's men buy the remaining lots. I left unpossessed by any new possessions, but with a whole complex of things to think about.

What was he talking about? I knew, and didn't know. Yes, he and I had been talking for years, somewhere in that dimension below consciousness where the lilac and honeysuckle bloomed. My life had gone by in a blur, while those bushes pushed forth their distinctive edges and colors, gave off those perfumes year after year. If you don't know what I'm talking about, forget it. But it's part of the story, an essential part. There are friends you've been talking to for years, without knowing it, but knowing it. In my case, one of those friends was with me again, our voices no longer bodiless but made up of real sounds, real inflections. That maple light had touched us again. The brick building was real again. It was as though I'd awakened after an hour's sleep after Vic and I had spent all night listening to our records, as we had so often.

I had a dream that night. I was kneeling in a batter's circle as the scene around me became clear. Lime smell, crowd noises increasing, the infield and dugouts appearing from drizzle and fog. I was in pinstripes. Mantle had just walked, his luminous number 7 floating by me on the way to first. The walk had moved Vic over to second. . . .

I could hear Vic yelling, "Knock us in, Billy, do it." Walking to the plate, I told myself what I'd always told myself when I was at bat, just a simple chant to myself to help me concentrate, something short, direct, something to help me focus: *"If* it's a strike, hit it, hard." I was in the batter's box, my right heel against the back line. "*If* it's a strike, hit it, hard. . . ."

Vic and the Mick had their leads. The infield grass was lush and wet, a deep green, almost black. There was a rosebush between short and third, thick brambles, beautiful and full roses, but I was confident that I could drive a ball through it. I was ready. The roses were like faces in a crowd. Vic's imploring voice above the intensifying crowd roar. I was ready. But where was the pitcher?

7

For the first time tonight, Vic is in Elvis's room. Eddie Rogas just stopped by, poured me some coffee from the thermos that his wife, Lynne, packs him every night. We didn't talk.

We listened as Elvis wondered if the woman he still loved gazed at her doorstep and pictured him there. Coming from upstairs, Elvis's voice sounded as though it was passing through ten tombs before it got to us. Eddie didn't notice, didn't sense Vic's mood.

Eddie wanted to be friendly, to patch things up. But I brushed him off, and didn't touch the coffee.

Last night, about midnight, while Eddie and I were sipping coffee together, the red button on my desk lit up and both of us walked up to the third floor. Vic was in his room. He didn't have any music on. He couldn't sleep, he said, and offered us a drink. Vic and I had scotch and water, Eddie a beer. Just to make small talk, Vic asked Eddie how Lynne was taking to being at home again, but didn't give Eddie a chance to answer, saying, "I bet she's relieved." He said he hoped Lynne didn't mind Eddie's hoot owl shift here at the school. Eddie said she didn't, and then said something dumb and wounding, though Vic strained not to let on he'd been hit. Eddie said, "The money's good ..." and tried to cut himself off, but his stupidity had blundered through again. I wanted to punch him in his flat imbecile's freckled face, grab him by his long red hair, and throw him out of the building. I made up my mind to talk to Vic about Eddie. I'd been through this before, somewhere else. I wasn't going to go through it again. Eddie had never understood. He never would.

I'm still exhausted, I guess, from everything that's happened. The last few days, after my shift, after doing as much night-dreaming as writing, I've gotten back to my apartment by a little after eight, scrambled myself a couple of eggs, and dropped off into a hard sleep, phone off the hook, air conditioner hum drowning out the noise of Smithtown's traffic. I don't think I've ever slept this much or this hard before. A couple weeks of this and I might get my strength back, my resiliency, and be able to sort things out. I've always cared for the word "clarity," remember Miss Koch in Latin I talking about "claritas" (is that the word?). Whenever I think of the word I think somehow of distinct leaf edges, the toothed leaves of elm, chestnut.

I want to tell Vic's story simply, clearly. I wish I could do an outline and then just follow it all the way, but the story's still happening, so that wouldn't work. Also, I can see I've already learned some things from what I've already written. I don't know what the thing as a whole means, just that it *does* mean. I need to keep feeling my way along, getting things down as they occur to me.

The stuff I see in the papers, in the gossip magazines, the stuff I hear almost every night these days on television—it's off the mark even when it's well-meaning. I don't know where the bull's-eye is, but I do know whether arrows are purposely or

innocently missing it. Dan Rather's last segment a few nights
ago on CBS did it again: "Vic Holyfield, eccentric forty-eight-
year-old Texas multibillionaire, is still living in his old high
school on Long Island." The camera showed the front steps, the
facade ivy crawling up to and around the letters SMITHTOWN
HIGH SCHOOL. "Vic, as we've all come to call him, is
incommunicado, but a close friend reports that Vic is working
out a plan to buy the small college in Ohio where he spent his
freshman year and to do there next year what he did this past
year in Smithtown. Officials at Oberlin College have no
comment, though President Elkins said that so far as he knew
Oberlin is not for sale. Members of the Board of Trustees have
not been available for comment." The truth is, Dan, there's
about as much of a chance that anything like this has even
crossed Vic's mind as there is that the Mick will ever hit
another world series homer against a lefty pitcher by the name
of Shazam. Vic doesn't remember anything about Oberlin except
that it was a place to get away from. President Elkins can rest
easy.

8

A couple days after the auction, which was a few days before
Vic called me from Dallas, I walked over to the school. One of
Vic's men was sitting on the front steps. He kept his eye on me
as I made my slow way around the half-circle sidewalk from
New York Avenue to in front of him to back out to the street,
but we didn't talk, though he recognized me and we nodded to

each other. He asked me if there was anything he could do for me. I said no. If he hadn't been around, I'd probably have looked into the first-floor windows, or walked around out back. If Vic hadn't been at the auction, I'd have gone into the building that morning, walked down to the old gym. Maybe I'd have stood within the center circle, gotten something out of my system. But I knew that I'd see Vic soon, and that we'd look the building over together. He hadn't bought it just to sell it again. And he hadn't bought it as a luxury estate for the latest woman, Sophia Loren, he'd been linked with. No, Smithtown was not Sophia's Rome. If Vic were interested in her, he'd probably buy the Pantheon for her, and a few of Raphael's paintings to hang over the painter's bier there.

Vic's man would have taken me through the building, but I didn't want to walk those halls with him. I suppose it would have been okay with him if I'd wanted to walk through by myself, but I didn't want to ask him.

I didn't know why Vic had bought our old school, though I wasn't sure I believed him, exactly, when he'd said he didn't know what the hell he was doing at the auction. I knew I'd find out soon, and that would be soon enough.

I could smell autumn in the air that last week of August. It was already getting dark by around eight. I spent my evenings watching television. A couple baseball races were tight. I spent my evenings waiting for the other shoe to fall.

9

I remember that Vic called me on a Friday to say he'd visit
me the following Thursday evening. This was the Thursday
after Labor Day. He said he wanted to stay with me for a night.
I asked him if he was kidding, said I had only one bedroom. He
said no, he wasn't kidding, said I probably had an extra couch,
which I did. I told him to come on ahead, but that there
wouldn't be room for his bodyguards. He laughed and said they
could sleep in the car.

I spent days wondering what was on his mind, and how we
were going to connect. I wasn't doing anything, had given up
work months before, still felt brain-lame and burned out. But
was I ready to change my life? For one thing, I knew that I
could be rich in a minute: all I had to do was to ask Vic to set
me up. But I couldn't have asked him, of course. But I did
think of it, thought of spending my life gambling in Monte
Carlo or staring out at the sea from a lighthouse off the coast of
Ireland, or of just getting out of Smithtown, drifting back down
south and talking to a few people I've wanted to ask a few
things. Well, I could do that anyway. Maybe Vic would want to
go with me. I'll never quite be able to describe this exactly, but
maybe one of the things that has kept Vic and me together over
the years is that while we were doing what we were doing, we
were really doing something else somewhere else. Now, maybe,
with Vic's power, spirit would rejoin body in some way I
couldn't yet understand.

I happened to be looking out the window of my apartment down onto Main Street when he arrived that Thursday afternoon. Carrying just a briefcase, he jumped out of his block-long Cadillac limousine as though he was thirty years late for our appointment. I could hear him pounding up the stairs between the barbershop and the office-supply store as though he'd been to my place before. I opened the door before he had a chance to knock.

He was pale, looked tired. "Jesus, these two weeks," he said. He was wearing jeans that looked slept-in, and a flannel shirt. He hadn't shaved in a day or two. But his blue eyes glinted. He went into the bathroom to splash his face.

We sat at the kitchen table, sipping scotch. One of his men brought in a basket of food, and left. Vic took my phone off the hook.

With each inch of scotch, I became less and less conscious of my old friend's celebrity. He became Vic for me again. Once in a while I asked a question, but in the main Vic talked, all that afternoon and night, into the early morning. We lay down, wiped out, at about six. I woke at noon. Vic was already gone. I'd see him about once a month for a year, he'd told me, and then I'd see him every day for a year.

We were going back, Vic said. We were going back to where our earth was back there in the '50s, into that very essence and curvature of starlight. As he spoke, I thought of quasars, their light coming to our eyes from 10 to 12 billion light-years away. The quasars themselves had perished, burned themselves out maybe 6 to 8 billion light-years ago, but the light kept coming toward us, a light of the distant past. Vic and I and our high school were in a much more recent light, and we were going to enter it again, he said, though he said it differently.

We would restore the building, with certain adjustments. We would live in it. We would contact our classmates—this would be easy, he said—and they would live in it with us, too. For a school year. He himself was a magnet, and his money was a magnet, he said, and it would be no problem getting our

classmates and key people from other classes to spend a year
with us. We would all have to live in the building, or the spell
could not weave itself, he said. He said there would be music
rooms instead of classrooms on the third floor. There would be
three of them: a ballad room, a room where faster rock and roll
would be played, and a room just for E. He said that instead of
attending classes, though there would be some lectures and
movies and discussions for people who wanted them, we'd go to
the music rooms. We would live here with a broad margin to
our lives, as there never was before, Vic said.

There would be gym shifts. We'd eat in the cafeteria, three
meals a day, though he'd often have special catering done. He
was still thinking through plans, getting better ideas every day.
We'd have a basketball team again, and a baseball team, and
we'd even compete again against some of the same players from
other towns we'd competed against in high school. Not to win
games, he said, but somehow to accept one another and
ourselves in what we in our bodies had become since the light
held us in its arms thirty years ago.

We'd have dances in the gym again. Maybe we'd make a
few trips together, but we couldn't stay away from the school
for long.

I told Vic that my older brother Werner once said to me,
"Billy, I swear that one of these days I'm going to pinch
myself and wake up back in high school."

"Yes, we'll want him and Barbara," Vic said. "We'll want our
best friends from other classes, too, and they'll want to do this
with us. The building is ours. If it weren't, I'd have to have a
replica built, you know. I'm going to do this," he said. "I need
you. I need to walk those halls again with that music in my
head. Do you remember Eddie Williams, Billy, the guy who
transferred in from the city? The first time I heard 'Earth
Angel' it was Eddie Williams singing it as he brought the ball
down court one practice. While he was dribbling! Do you
realize what that meant, what basketball and music were to us,
and how Eddie brought them together for me that day? I didn't

know then what I know now. I just knew that Eddie gave me the chills. And that night I heard 'Earth Angel' on the radio for the first time. I keep hearing Eddie singing it.

"Did you know Fats Domino wrote 'Earth Angel,' Billy? We'll have Fats visit us. We'll spend a year away from the Trident, the Straits of Ormuz, the abortion issue, Central America, space shuttles, all those fucking hijackings. We'll find things out. We'll slow time down. This time, we'll do it on our own terms.

"I've been haunted," he said. "I knew you'd listen and understand. I knew you'd be the one to make the faithful leap and see this through with me. Believe me, we can do it. The one thing I won't tolerate is disbelief. Our lives in our building again, day by day, will generate meaning. There will be empty spaces, but we and our old friends will be together again within that emptiness. We'll miss our other lives, but less and less as the weeks go by, you know. My money—I realized that I was rich enough to do *anything.* I realized I could go back to high school if I wanted to, go back to it in a way no one has ever gone back before. Never mind *Grease* and *American Graffiti* and all that shit we look at and listen to to help us dream our way back. Never mind the ending of *The Big Chill.* We are going back. We're about fifty fucking years old now, but we're going back. It was Margo who wrote me about the old building for sale. That's all she said. She sent a telegram from California to me in Dallas that said 'S.H.S. at auction August twenty-fourth.' That's all it said. I haven't seen her since the Thanksgiving after high school. I talked to her yesterday. She'd heard from Harold Molinoff here on the Island about the school. She knew she had to telegraph me, that I was the only one who would be able to do anything about it, the only one who would know what to do with the information. I told her I was planning things. Include her in, she said. Of course, I said. I told her that I had to work something out that in fact had a lot to do with her, and she didn't know it, but

she did, or she wouldn't have telegraphed me, Billy, you know,"
he said.

Vic talked like this all night long. I didn't tape record this, of
course, so my direct quotes are not really quotes, but that's the
best I can do. Gradually, I began to understand. There were no
limits. He'd built enough hospitals, sent enough care packages
to undernourished nations, he said. He said he was going to be
selfish. He was not going to go through the rest of his life
habitually, squandering it, as though the life of business and
progress and the stock market and new home communications
and data-bank systems were what the universe was conspiring
toward as ultimate reality. Vic said that he lay awake some
nights on purpose so that he could use himself as his own
resource, could keep swirling down and into and under his
own thoughts, under the jumbles of figures and projections and
jargon of board-room language, to get down to how the mind
works, to what formed it, and he was convinced that at the
center somewhere we were still alive in all our motives and
motions at once, that the worlds were simultaneous, and our
year back in high school would prove this.

He said he'd once had a dream: it was the end of the world,
a nuclear cloud moving across the country like a curtain, and
he was back in Smithtown, huddled in the gym with all of us,
and he was happy that he would be dying this way, here, with
us. In waking life he had been trying to stay alive, he said, but
it hadn't been easy—too many leaning on him, the oppressive
phones even in his limos and planes. Shocks were already going
through his empire, he said. He'd told his $200,000-a-year
gophers that he was dropping away for a time. They thought he
was going crazy. He'd sold some land, liquidated a few
businesses over the past two weeks, put others in charge of the
rest. He said he was making so much money even as we spoke
that we could never spend it that fast—his arms moved up and
down like Texas pumpjacks, then twirled like the blades of
harvesters in Kansas wheatfields. He said that if it was true
that all the gold ever refined would amount to a cube about

the size of a large barn, then he had in his vaults the haymow, at least. He said that now he was going to buy enough of time back so that he would have a chance to live inside his soul again. He believed that he could buy Time itself. It didn't come in a bottle, he said. It came inside the place where we were once most alive, and we would breathe the air of that place again, he swore.

He spoke in images of transistors and flash interstices and synapse electricity that I didn't follow. I didn't have to. I'd heard what happened to his voice when he mentioned Margo, when he spoke of Elvis and our first music.

10

I wrote that last part last night. As I mentioned, I would have needed a tape recorder that early morning two years ago to get it all right, but I think I've got the gist of it for you. Vic was settling things fast. We had come together, as both of us, during our clearest moments over thirty years, knew we would. His genius, he said, had been a means toward that end.

I've done some thinking since last night about Margo, but have nothing to say right now. Not even to myself. Later, maybe, but no promises to myself or you. She's a heavy presence in this building right now, though she's not here and I don't know where she is and don't particularly want to know. But for his sake I hope Vic knows.

Very quiet in the building tonight. Vic is upstairs—I know this because I saw his limo out at the gate and his helicopter on the roof when I came in—but I don't hear any music. He may be in his darkroom, developing pictures of the past year. Or he may be on the phone with Margo.

He fired Eddie Rogas. He told me he told Eddie he'd be better off at home with Lynne and the kids. He gave Eddie a year's severance pay.

I don't think we'll need anyone to take Eddie's place. Three of Vic's bodyguards man the gate and patrol the fence he built around the whole property. Gawkers circle this place and peer in as though it were the White House or Graceland Mansion, but things are secure and generally quiet here. I'd just as soon have the night shift to myself, but this is up to Vic, of course.

Mid-September now, two years since work began on the school, one year since the return began.

11

I woke at noon the day after my talk with Vic. He was already gone. He called a couple evenings later from Switzerland, told me that work crews from Dallas would be arriving at the end of September, that they'd have plans with them for the renovations, but that he'd appreciate it if I'd check over at the school on the work to see that it all *felt* right. It had to be done well inside a year, he said. The crews would have definite instructions, but my word was law, he said. He told me I could hire and fire, could tell the crews when to jump and how high, could call in anybody from anywhere at any time for advice or to get work done.

He said that one of his financial managers would be moving into Smithtown, that I had an open checkbook, and he meant *open.* He said that money was nothing, and that the only thing he asked me—he said he wished he were with me so that he could look into my eyes as he said this—was that I not consider the cost. Money was illusion, he said, unless it created life. He'd be in town when he could be, but by Thanksgiving at the latest. He said a woman, his executive secretary from Dallas, would be moving to Smithtown and in touch with me within a week. He said he was thinking about me and our work all day and all night long even when he was thinking or dreaming about something else. He said he knew I knew what he meant.

His secretary knocked on my door three or four days later. She was carrying several Smithtown High School yearbooks. She seemed to be as shy as I was. She introduced herself as Ellen Weaver. She'd been with Mr. Holyfield for twenty-one years.

I felt attracted to Ellen right away. I hadn't been with a woman, even this close to a woman, in a long time, and when we pulled up kitchen chairs together, I knew I'd have a hard time paying attention. But I was surprised at myself, too. After what I'd been through, for a long time I thought all my emotions were on hold.

She began talking, turning yearbook pages, but then, when she saw me looking sidelong at her, asked me, "You don't remember me, do you?" "No," I said, but at that instant *did,* or at least I recognized her, somehow. College? Down south?

She had gray eyes. Her figure, even beneath a gray business suit, was heartbreaking. She wore her blond hair in a modified Lady Di cut. I'd have remembered. But, no, I didn't know her.

"We were classmates," she said. "Ellen Mulloy. You probably didn't know me, but I knew you." She opened our senior yearbook and pointed to her picture. I did vaguely remember the mousy little thing in the picture. She wore eyeglasses then, wore contacts now, and that was the least of the changes. "I don't know why I didn't tell you right away," she said. "I thought maybe Vic had told you."

Vic had let Ellen be a surprise to me. She was somehow already a sign that everything was possible.

We went out to dinner, spoke most of the time about Vic. Then I spent several hours with her and her two secretaries at their rooms in the Smithtown Hotel. They'd had extra phones installed. They already had school records, mementoes of reunions, class lists. They began calling members of my class, and some friends I mentioned who had been in other classes. Their message to those they caught in—and they got through to dozens right while I was sitting there—was simple: each of them could expect an important letter from Mr. Victor Holyfield within a month. If possible, they should not make any plans for the ten months beginning the following September before hearing from Mr. Holyfield. Warm regards from their old friends Vic and Ellen and yours truly.

I called Werner myself. What the hell is going on, Billy? he asked me. That's all I could tell him right now, I told him. I told him he'd be damned sorry if he and Barbara made any other plans for those ten months. I told him that about next September he could pinch himself.

I left Ellen at about midnight. I was shaken. I had to walk around town for an hour to catch my breath. Things were going too fast for me, but this time people were in control.

It was all going to happen. I wasn't dreaming. I walked past the school. It waited back there in the trees like an imploded star.

12

Roofers, painters, electricians, plumbers, carpenters, moved into town. A gardener was there to rake leaves and lay in bulbs and prune the shrubs—he said he'd been with Mr. Holyfield for fifteen years, and would be staying on the Island now until Mr. Holyfield left. He'd be in charge of flowers for the whole building. Tony Piccione is his name. He's still around.

The work crews knew what they were doing. I was more than welcome among them, but minded my business except for a few small things—paint colors, memorabilia in the display cases outside the old science rooms on the second floor, restoration of the fifty-year-old gym clock rather than installation of a new but very different model—and one big one. More on that later. It would be a surprise for Vic. I kept my fingers crossed that it would please him. He'd see my touch on opening day. When I saw him at Thanksgiving that fall while the work was being done on the school, I asked him to stay out of the auditorium.

By then Ellen and I were not putting on Vic or ourselves. We were caught up in this, and our enthusiasm made Vic glad. Each time he arrived on the scene again, he was at first doubtful and sheepish, but when he heard from Ellen and me, he began talking again as he had that night in my apartment. And he in turn excited me and Ellen all over again, in case any doubts had crept in.

Vic also bought Nick's, our sweet shop two blocks down on

25

Main Street. It was still in business. It was laid out like
Arnold's in *Happy Days* now, with an open square in the center,
but would be restored back to what it was, Vic said, old
rainbow Seaburg jukebox, booths, ceiling fans, and all. It
wouldn't be open all the time, but Ellen would work an
occasional lunch or evening party there into the schedule.

I saw Ellen more than often that year, but we kept it to
business. She knew a little bit of what I'd been through, had
probably heard about it from Vic. Also, we were both burned
shy, and both amazed at what we were doing for and with
Vic.

By the first of November she and her staff had moved their
office into where the school's main office had always been,
down in the center of the first floor. Their desks were behind
the high counter that I had come to so often for a late pass.
The windows in this room looked out to the front lawn under
the maples where I'd stood with Vic at the auction. Now I
was inside looking out again. I didn't need a pass, and I didn't
have to worry about any tests. In many ways—never mind my
jock image in high school—I'd just been a scared kid, worried
about the future, intimidated by some of the teachers—the
ones who wanted to intimidate us, like old Claffey, who was
always talking about his sacred master's degree. I would like
my old self and "master" Claffey to rest in peace.

Once in a while Ellen would call me to the phone to say hello
to a classmate. I hated this, but thought it necessary for my
own sake, thought it would help break the ice toward when I'd
be meeting them again. Some of them were filled with
questions; some just gushed uncontrollably and asked me if I
was really me and if Vic was really behind this whole thing.
By then, they'd all gotten Vic's same initial letter, the whole
class, even those that Vic and I hadn't really known. Ellen sent
my copy to my apartment address. She knew I'd be flabbergasted,
even though I already knew generally what was in it. I've kept
the letter. This is it:

November 1, 1987

Dear Billy,

You and our other classmates have been more in my thoughts than you could have supposed. I'm glad, now, that we've made contact again. But I'll save the niceties for later, when we meet again, and get down right away to what I have in mind.

I've purchased our old New York Avenue high school in Smithtown. My work crews are now at the school restoring it to what it was when you and I walked those halls. Most classrooms, though, will be turned into living quarters, and I invite you to live in the building with me and many—I hope all—of our old classmates for a school-year-long reunion. Please plan to arrive in Smithtown a day or two before Labor Day next September so that you can settle in. First day of "school" is the first day of that next week.

If you are married, your spouse is welcome. If you have children still at home with you, I'm afraid you'll have to make other arrangements for them, but I expect this will affect only one or two of you, if any. My secretary, Ellen Mulloy, Smithtown High School Class of 1957, will be in touch with you regarding any special requirements you might have—don't be afraid to let her and her staff know of any particular health or diet needs, any special facilities you might need to make your 9½-month stay with us happy and comfortable—and will enclose a contract for you (and your spouse if applicable) to sign.

Thank you. Please feel free to call Ellen with any questions. (Her numbers are 516-AN5-4100, 4101, 4102.) Hoping to see you in September.

Vic Holyfield

Vic's letter, of course, hadn't told anybody what the hell they'd be doing there in the school for nine-and-a-half months. Not that I knew, either. The letter was necessarily general,

and mysterious enough. I doubt that many of our friends slept
much for a few nights, or even for ten months, after reading
it.

My contract was enclosed. Vic was offering me and each
schoolmate $250,000, to be paid in ten monthly installments of
$25,000 each, to come back to high school. A quarter of a
million dollars each. An offer almost no one could refuse, or
would want to. John Johahnsen, a realtor in East Quogue on the
Island, told me later that the money was nothing otherworldly
for him, but that he would have signed the contract for nothing.
Eddie Rogas asked if he and Lynne would have to pay for
their food at the school.

The contract is much too long and rambling for me to
reproduce it here. I haven't looked at it in a long time. In any
case, it was probably dictated by Vic into a machine while he
was fatigued and maybe even half in a scotch haze above the
clouds. Ellen probably tightened it up for him as best she could
in light of Vic's rush to get it into the mail. Vic wanted
something, some kind of agreement in writing that would
make us take the whole thing seriously, though I doubt that
such a contract would hold up in court, not that Vic would ever
push it that far. The contract keeps referring to "the spirit of
the occasion," asking that we enter into a pact against time, and
return. It asks us if we remember the first time we heard the
Five Satins sing "In the Still of the Night," and asks us to listen
to it again as we think over the contract. It tells us we will be
entertained, deepened, "relumed," in the spirit of the '50s and
that this year of ours together "for which we here in the right
spirit join our signatures for contract" would be a year, as Ralph
Waldo Emerson said, that would add to our store of time
rather than diminish it. (I'm no literary critic, but it doesn't take
one to know that sometimes Vic speaks in two or three voices
at once.) The contract has few details. We would follow our
own geniuses, and would not be misled in doing so, the
contract says. It asks us to agree to sign out for any overnights,
letting Ellen and staff know, but that in "the spirit of the

occasion" we would be expected in the main to make our alma
mater our residence.

I signed my contract with a John Hancock flourish and sent it
in. I got back a copy countersigned by Vic, the i's, so help me,
dotted with happy-faces. Don't take this the wrong way: this
was a locker-room joke from the old days, those faces
appearing one day you know where to the delight of our
teammates.

The fat return envelopes began arriving in Ellen's office. I'd
lean on the counter and hear her sing out from day to day,
"Three today, Billy," or "Four today." Every time I walked
home from her office or from watching the building take the
form Vic had outlined for his workmen, I wondered if I would
wake up from all this.

The local papers learned something was up. I got calls every
day, but just referred the callers to Vic. They'd never get
through to him, of course. I felt as though I were taking the
Fifth Amendment on the whole thing, but took my lead from
Vic. If he wanted a press conference, he'd call one.

Some of our old friends dropped off their contracts
themselves. I stayed scarce at those times, disappeared. I
wanted to experience the return as completely as Vic did.

Ellen also began to hear from S.H.S. graduates who hadn't
been in our class, people we didn't know and hadn't contacted.
Some would confront her in her office. Ellen had to bring in a
couple of Vic's men, men in shades who looked like the Blues
Brothers with muscles, to screen visitors or escort them out.
There were some distasteful scenes. But we didn't have room
for everybody.

Ellen gave me an American Express card, authorized by Vic.
I had unlimited funds, she said. Mr. Till, the financial man
who had moved into Smithtown from Dallas, no doubt
scratching his bald and baffled head all the way, would take
care of the monthly bills. By the way, Ellen said, Vic had
purchased my Smithtown apartment for me in my name. She

said that Vic mentioned to her that he hoped and trusted that I
wouldn't mind.

I would like to report that at this point I felt offended, as
though my freedom were being taken away from me. But I
didn't. It's not only that I remembered and had taken to heart
my friend Vic's one injunction, that I not pay attention to
money. The truth is that I didn't/don't give a shit about money.
It has nothing to do with my inner life. Elvis knew this about
himself, but didn't know that he knew it.

I didn't mind not having to bother about money. My
unemployment checks had stopped. My old Chevy had
grunted its last, so I charged a goddamned new Buick to Vic,
and I knew that this would please him, as it did. He told me,
when I saw him that first Thanksgiving—so help me, he had
tears in his eyes as he said this—that it had been a gift to him
when he learned that I'd gotten that car. He thanked me. He
said he knew the spirit in which I'd purchased the car. He
said he knew he and I were in all this together all the rest of
the way, that my getting the car had reassured him, had taken
a weight off his mind. This was not a novel we were living, he
said, one in which the novelist needs a conflict so invents one
where there wouldn't otherwise have been one. This was our
life, and we both knew what was important. A gift to him, he
said. He gave me a set of Elvis cassettes for the car's tape player.
He knew it was a dangerous thing for him to do. "Just chuck
them away, Billy, if you want," he said, "but I thought maybe
... maybe E is getting a kick out of all this by now, pun
intended."

Maybe half the work on the building was done by
Thanksgiving, when Vic and Ellen and I had turkey, just for
fun, in the cafeteria—Ellen had arranged for the dinner to be
driven out to us from one of Vic's favorite N.Y.C.
restaurants—and then toured the three floors. Vic's apartment
was on the third floor in the south corner, where Bernard
Skolsky had taught us English, or tried to. A loft had been built
into the high-ceilinged room, as it had in most others, so that

it had almost twice the space there would otherwise have been.
Vic said he had thought of busting through a wall and giving
himself what had been Mr. Erb's business education room, too,
but space in the building was limited, and he didn't want any
more than anybody else. The effect of his apartment, and every
other, was spacious, even though a small bathroom had been
partitioned off in each one. The plumbers and electricians had
to be geniuses for this job, Vic said. They were not allowed to
alter the outer shape of the building one whit.

I asked him what the whirligigs and weights were on a table
in one corner of his room. I noticed, too, vials of mercury,
magnets, coils of wire. "Billy, I'm embarrassed to say," he said,
"I'm screwing around with a perpetual motion machine." If
he's gotten anywhere with it since, I haven't heard a word about
it.

On the second floor we passed what would be Doc Saunders'
double office. Doc was Vic's personal physician from Texas,
and would be joining us in the fall, living here, giving out
placebos, Vic said. We also looked in on a double room being
fitted in the space above the auditorium. It was to be for one
of Vic's special friends, someone who would be in and out. I
don't want to play games with you here, so I'll tell you right
now. This was being done for Phil Spector, who appeared and
disappeared like a ghost off and on last year. He'd rather I
included him out of this accounting, maybe. Wispy and
stilt-heeled, he jangled by once in a while. I don't even think
my classmates knew he was around. I only spoke with him a
few times—rather, he spoke at me. He didn't know anything
about me, and didn't want to.

My own apartment was all the way down the hall opposite
Vic's, in the north corner, where the library had been. Vic
stood in front of my inscribed photographs of Elvis for a long
time.

Ellen's room was next to mine. I didn't know who had
assigned the rooms, though I suspected that she had, and I
didn't ask. But the fact that our two rooms were close together

worried me, distracted me, for reasons that would be hard to explain. But I was only inventing a problem, somehow thinking that the year of the return should be kept free from any entanglements. I can't even write straight about whatever I was thinking at the time. I already more than cared for Ellen, and as it turned out I was just being a fool.

Downstairs, we passed by the auditorium. I had curtains over the windows in the doors. I had Vic by the elbow and steered him past.

Ellen reported to Vic. Of seventy-seven members of the Class of 1957, seven were "deceased," as she put it. One person, Eddie Williams in fact, had disappeared from his last known address in Florida. A detective was tracking him down. Contact by phone and certified letter had been made with all sixty-nine remaining. Signed contracts had been received from sixty-one of these. There would probably be more acceptances. Nineteen others altogether from the classes of 1956, 1958, and 1959 had been invited, and seventeen had already accepted. Altogether, including spouses, we could count on 110 to 130 people on hand for the opening. There were enough apartments being prepared, and she would plan on a few extras, including a couple of larger ones for visitors.

It was evening. The three of us were standing in front of the school on the top step. Vic looked up at the three words incised in marble above the doors, then looked up higher, into the skies. Ellen and I looked at Vic. He was beaming. It was all coming to be. I don't know if I'd ever before seen a man this happy.

His limo was purring below us. Vic had to leave for Kennedy and a flight to Dallas that night, had to fight the traffic to the city, rich as he was, until his helicopter pad could be installed.

As he got into the limo, I told him to take care of himself, told him that there were many of us now depending on him.

Ellen and I waved good-by to Vic. Then I walked her to the lobby of the Smithtown Hotel.

We squeezed hands good night. I wanted to kiss her, but

didn't, even though she may have wanted me to. As I said, it was somehow as though I didn't want to spoil anything. But this isn't something I can explain. Vic had obviously been glad that he had brought Ellen and me together, so the question of his relationship with her had nothing to do with this. In fact, Ellen told me later on that she and Vic had never been lovers. I guess I just didn't want this dream I was now entering to be disrupted by something I couldn't control. But that wasn't the whole thing. Another part of it was that there had been too many women throwing themselves at me for too long, women who would do anything just to get close to Elvis. I now wanted a different life. I may even have wanted the power of celibacy for myself that certain martial arts masters talk about. I truly believed that there was such a power, and that it was my lack of experience in that realm of denial that had kept me from finishing the training manual that I'd begun to write.... Anyway, I was going back now into something, going back into it with Ellen and Vic. I wanted to be a different person for this. But I wanted to be with Ellen, too, so kicked myself all the way back to my apartment for being so reluctant, or shy, or afraid, or silly, or whatever it was that kept me from falling in love—I guess *that* was it—with this perfect woman.

I couldn't sleep. I walked all the way down alongside the Jericho Turnpike to the Smithtown bull, Whisper, who stands above the traffic in his metal being. Richard "Bull" Smith had founded the town in the seventeenth century by trading with the Indians some trinkets for as much land as he could encircle, riding Whisper bareback, from sunrise to sunset, in one day. It was the story of Manhattan in miniature, with a dream action thrown in besides. Whisper was massive above me, glared out at the car lights that strobed him. His cock had been painted about ten colors, from red to aluminum—by high school kids, probably, as we'd painted it in my day. His cock flashed luridly out of the darkness. I sat below him, watching the traffic go by, imagining cars and trucks as the deer and bear of this new world.

13

It's two in the morning. Vic just stopped by my station. I could hear him coming down the stairs from the third floor, his footsteps echoing all the way.

"Are you okay?" I asked him.

"I'm okay."

"What's up?"

"Nothing. I'm going for a walk. I've got some business shit to think about. . . . Billy, I'm okay, really. My only worry, you know, is that you and Ellen worry about me too much."

He went outside and then came back in for a second to tell me he had some photographs to show me. He'd put them on my desk tomorrow. He asked me if I was doing all right without Rogas around.

"I'm doing better," I said.

He smiled. "Me, too," he said. "The place feels better, more like home."

So, I'm alone here. Vic won't come by this way when he comes in. He uses the back entrance. Sometimes he'll go down to the gym and shoot some baskets before going to bed. You can hear the bounce of the ball all the way here to where I'm sitting. I know that lately he wants to be alone, and I don't bother him, though I've stood in the dark on the balcony above one side of the gym and watched him. He changes into his shorts and sneakers, lights up only half the court. He moves around in a semicircle, hitting most of his jumpers, following in for a lay-up when he misses, then moving out again. He does some push-ups and sit-ups. When he's done he either takes a swim or walks upstairs to shower, maybe plays a record or two in one of the music rooms, and goes to bed.

14

Sooner or later, if I am going to be honest with this, I'm going to have to talk about Margo. I'll go back to the beginning, and get the misery over with. It's not as though some terrible skeleton is rattling around in the closet. It's just that it's not much fun thinking back on incidents that were so confusing at the time, and maybe embarrassing now.

Margo was the first girl I ever went to bed with. I was her first boy. Actually, it happened on the reclining seats of her parents' Rambler.

It was the summer of 1957, after we had all graduated. She'd picked me up so we could go together to visit Vic in the hospital in Port Jefferson. Vic had been sent there by a doctor who thought he had polio. Then, a spinal tap or two later, he was treated for meningitis. Then it turned out he had a dangerous strain of encephalitis. It could have killed him, but he got away with only a very slight hearing loss in one ear.

Margo and I drove to Port Jeff almost every evening all that August. She was his girl and I was his best friend. After seeing Vic, we'd drive back to Smithtown and park in the lot over by the baseball diamond at school to talk. We'd done this many times. We'd listen to the radio and sometimes catch Alan

Freed's program from New York. It was on that program that
I first heard several of Elvis's records. In fact, I remember Freed
once mentioning that he'd had requests from hundreds of
listeners to have Elvis appear at one of the shows in New York
City, but Elvis was already out of his price range, Freed said.
When it happened, it happened awfully fast.

She wore Vic's ring on a gold chain around her neck, and
fingered it as she talked about how skinny Vic had gotten,
how she was afraid he was going to die, how she'd had a dream
that Vic was in an open casket on his hospital bed and looked
like our classmate Bob Latchen who had been killed in an
automobile accident that May. The truth is, I think, that
Margo was now just visiting the hospital out of loyalty, maybe
friendship—she was probably repulsed by her boyfriend, his
pallid face and stick limbs, as most young girls would be. I
could tell you more about that, but won't. . . . We're only
human. We were not born fifty years old.

We began to hold hands, then sat closer, her head on my left
shoulder, on my chest. I kissed her hair, at first without her
knowing it. Then she began to know it, and one evening lifted
her face to mine for our first kiss. We broke away. It had been
an accident of some kind, and it wasn't going to happen again,
of course, not while our friend Vic was so sick, not ever; we
both loved Vic too much. Kids are filled with so much
melodrama.

A few evenings later, Vic was at home, recovering. I walked
over to see him. Margo was there. She and I left Vic's
together, maybe out of habit from the hospital visits, but also
because we wanted to and knew we would.

So that evening we became, for the first and only time,
"lovers." I have to laugh, though it was anything but funny at
the time. We were awkward, and felt guilty. Mainly, it hurt.

Imagine the scene around Vic's bed the next evening. I was
ashamed to be there talking with the two of them, trying to
pretend that nothing had happened. Margo was probably
wondering whether the whole world could tell by her face that

she was no longer a virgin. I left Vic's before Margo did, and we didn't have any plans to meet, and we never did again.

I sometimes try to imagine what her visits with Vic were like after that, and what Vic must have felt that August and when he went away to Oberlin. Maybe she told Vic about us. I don't know how close they were when they went away to college. I never wanted to ask. Maybe, for all I know, Vic spent the last weeks of the summer listening over and over to "That's When Your Heartaches Begin." Do you know the place in that record where Elvis moans?—you have to listen very close to hear it.

I remember that Margo and I exchanged addresses by phone—I was leaving Smithtown too. We wrote each other for a time, but our letters were all chatter of high school and Vic, as though that night in her parents' car hadn't happened and didn't matter. Maybe, for all I knew for sure, it hadn't happened. Maybe I hadn't even managed to do what I'd thought I did! I guess I wish I hadn't. In any case, it's a silly-ass thing even to bother to regret this many years later. But I keep wondering what it must have been like for Vic that summer. But I doubt that I'll ever ask him, or that he'll talk about that. We have to keep some things to ourselves, no matter what. Margo wrote me that she'd wanted to give Vic his ring back, but Vic didn't want it. He asked her to bury it for him.

Margo and I were seventeen. We were children. To tell the truth, sex scared the hell out of us. The culture made us into such children. Now, most of us have struggled all our lives to grow up, but everything around us encourages us to remain children, and almost all of us do. This was one of the main things that Vic was worried about while he was preparing for the return here to Smithtown High School of the Class of 1957. He was, plain and simple, worried about how childish he was being and asking us to be.

15

Vic checked in with Ellen and me about once a month. The
work on the building was going fast. The three of us would
tour the building, Ellen with her pad to note down any ideas.
It's surprising what you can think of to do when money, far
from being a problem, is not even a consideration. Do you want
a six-foot aquarium room divider filled with angelfish put in
between two areas of the lounge? Done.

After Vic's Smithtown visit in December, the three of us were
driven in his limo into New York for dinner at Rodney
Dangerfield's club. Vic hadn't said where we were going, so I
was still in jeans and sweatshirt, but it didn't matter—the
waiters bowed and scraped away in front of the Holyfield party.
No movie star, not even Sinatra, had Vic's power to part the
seas. Maybe not even Elvis.

As always after we had toured the high school, I was too
spaced out to taste food. I may have had a steak. Ellen said
that the food and wine here were fine but that maybe we should
have eaten in the cafeteria again. Vic said she was right, as
always.

Rodney, old pop-eyes, came over to our table, said he never
got any respect, said he'd gotten into an elevator that morning
and the operator had taken one look at him and said, "Going
down?" Said his wife had asked him the same thing on their
wedding night. The three of us laughed politely during
Rodney's riffles, but we were too distracted. Whatever it was

we were doing out in Smithtown, it wasn't funny, even as it
was.

The truth is that there were always too many people trying to
make Elvis laugh. He was the only one taking his music
seriously. It was just fucking impossible for him to grow with
his music because of all the jokesters around him. There was a
time, once he was done making those movies, once he swore
them off, that he was writing songs, planning an album of
quiet ballads to be backed by the Jordanaires again, but the
Colonel and others—well, let's just say that they had their own
version of what kind of product Elvis was going to be, and he
didn't have the spiritual strength to buck them. He didn't
have the *language*. Know what I mean? You can't even have a
thought without the word. I'm not an educated man, but I
know this: if you can't even put your own problems into words,
you can't deal with them. The truth is that Elvis and his
parents (when his mother was still alive) and his wife were
confused, scattered. You could see what was inevitable. His
role-playing and phoniness were tearing him apart, and he had
no one to articulate this for him. The atmosphere at Graceland
was that of an ongoing hysterical dream fantasy. I say this as a
participant, not an accuser. Enough.

Vic left from the Apple that night, but sent us home in his
limo. On the drive back out to the Island, Ellen and I huddled
close in the backseat. I asked her if she had known Vic and
visited him that summer Vic had been in the hospital. She
knew him, she said, but not well enough to visit. She'd been one
of those people in every class who had blended into the lockers
and woodwork and books, she said, not like Margo, captain of
the cheerleaders, not like "the great and privileged members of
the caste of jocks."

She always had fun putting me on like this. Her voice is
throaty and musical. "God, Billy, you were impressive," she
said. "In your red-and-white Smithtown Indian shorts. I can't
wait to see you in them again." I told her to knock it off. "I
went to every game. You made the first basket in the

championship game. Maybe you made them all." She had me
blushing again. I was glad it was dark.

"Ellen," I asked, "is there any hope for me?" She knew what
I meant. "Billy," she asked, "is there any hope for any of us?"
Then she answered herself—"I hope not"—and we both
laughed.

She told me that the year before in Dallas she'd found our
senior yearbook on Vic's desk. When he came into the room
he told her, sharply, to put it down. It may have been the only
time that Vic was ever short with her, or angry. He
apologized right away. It was just that he'd felt a quick stab of
embarrassment, Vic Holyfield of Dallas, the world's executive,
caught with his high school yearbook on his desk.

We drove the Long Island Expressway in the left lane, our
driver sliding us past the sparse early-morning traffic. We
could see other drivers in dashboard glow, but they couldn't see
us past the limo's one-way windows. I thought of the pools of
streetlamp light along the highway as light-years through which
we were passing, back to home, back to school, borne back on
the green wings of Vic's money to where our earth had been
when we were teenagers.

16

I was in charge of stocking the films for our theater, and the
books for our library. Vic told me, apologetically, that his
favorite films were, in this order, *Dr. Zhivago* (the boy seeing
leaves falling into his mother's grave, the poet writing *The*

Lara Poems during that winter at Varykino, Omar Sharif losing
Lara, if it was her, in a crowd), *Sayonara* (Brando waiting
beyond the bridge for his geisha love), *On the Beach* ("a movie
that should bring us together before the cloud does"), and *To
Sir, With Love* (when the children of the London ghetto learn to
love Poitier, Vic said, something cried out in him every
time—he imagined himself, someday, being a teacher in such a
school, teaching the kids to make a tossed salad or to repair a
radio). Oh, he liked Bogie, and some foreign films, and *Gone
With the Wind* and James Dean, but we'd been talking of
movies that somehow hit us from somewhere beyond what they
seemed to be about. Vic said that the emotional key to the *Star
Trek* television series and the movies was the "family on the
bridge" as it moved through the dangers of the future. He
didn't want to triple-guess himself, he said. He knew what hit
him.

As it turned out, though, I doubt that he watched more than
a movie or two all year.

I didn't buy any of those horrible rock-and-roll flicks, of
course, the ones that had been shown between shows at the
Fox and Paramount, or any of those beach things. We would
never be kids again, Vic said. We were not aiming for
"verisimilitude," he said. We didn't have to relive all our asinine
times. We could be selective.

I didn't stock Elvis's films, except for *Jailhouse Rock* and *King
Creole,* but did get in good documentaries on Buddy Holly and
others.

I don't have much of a stomach for books anymore, but hired
Mr. Gillman, our old librarian, who was still around serving as
Smithtown Town Historian, to outfit our library, to do
whatever he wanted. The small room wouldn't be where it
was in the old days, but he'd be in charge. I had Mr. Till
contact Gillman to work out a deal. Gillman wouldn't live in
the school, but would be on hand a few hours each day, one of
several of our teachers who would spend time at the school.
Maybe they would make us feel younger than we were. They

always seemed ancient to us anyway, and while they were still
alive they stood between us and our graves.

I gave Gillman the go-ahead to have a fireplace put in a
corner of his library. It made for a cozy spot, and he always
had someone there to sip sherry with, to talk over the great
books, to read to. Without those pain-in-the-ass students
around, high school was a joy for him.

Then it was time.

In August of 1988 Vic moved into his room. I'd already
moved in, as had Ellen.

We had the last meetings, Mr. Till and Tony Piccione and
various contractors and food personnel and security people
sitting in with Ellen and Vic and me at various times, usually in
Vic's office, which was adjacent to Ellen's on the first floor.

"Can anyone think of any loose thread?" Vic asked at our last
meeting. I couldn't. No one could. I remember a long silence
when Vic dreamed away to somewhere. . . .

Our guests would be moving in over the Labor Day weekend.
Their rooms were ready down to every shag rug and drape.
Trunks had preceded many of them and were waiting for them
in their rooms. A bowl of fresh fruit and an arrangement of
old Tony's flowers would be placed in each room the night
before the arrival.

On reunion eve, the three of us walked the halls for an hour,
looked into rooms, stood by the pool looking into the
blue-black water. We went down to the gym, and sat at a table
under the balcony. A waiter appeared. We drank two bottles
of wine by candlelight there in the corner of our old gym.

Vic had us hold hands around the table. He said a short
prayer: "Lord, let it be well with us." Then Vic and I walked
Ellen back to her room. Vic dropped me off at mine. There was
nothing left to say. I watched him walk down the dark hall to
his room, head down, hands in his pockets, sort of nodding to
himself. *Now*, I'm going to wake up, I told myself, this is the
moment, *now*. And that night, for the first time, Ellen unlocked
my door and came to me in bed.

17

The three of us were on hand as our old friends began to arrive, but we lay low, letting them settle in and marvel. Ellen's staff showed them to their rooms, and handed out schedules and menus, information on Doc's office, lists of names and short biographies of all those who would be with us. There was a phone in every room, and Vic would pay for all phone calls all year long.

A dozen porters moved with luggage from the semicircle in front of the school through the three sets of doors. We were blessed with a warm and sunny day. The maples would soon be red and yellow, would lose their leaves, but the world, Vic said, would always wear the colors of our spirit.

The contract said something about no pets, but Margie Eaton had a parrot that Vic spoke to. Ratch Casano looked like Easy Rider and wanted to ride his cycle up to his room, but one of Ellen's good-looking hostesses showed Ratch the wisdom and security of the garages out behind the school. Ralph and Edie Thompson (both Class of '57) felt they needed their grand piano, but Ellen had known about this, and had assigned them part of what had been the industrial arts room on the first floor—it had a ramp outside leading up to wide doors, and movers got the piano into their quarters easily.

Joe Quinlan arrived from Manhasset by bike. Marilyn Boschen's mother dropped her off, and wanted to stay with Marilyn—they lived together over in Jersey somewhere—but

Marilyn finally escaped. Don Pike, wearing a godawful
pitch-black wig, arrived from Wisconsin with Pat Jennehahn, his
old girl he hadn't seen since school. They'd gotten together by
phone after Vic's first letter, and he'd picked her up in
Cleveland on the way to Smithtown. If Don's wig bothered
Pat (*Pat, Pat,* I thought, *Pat,* and pictured her singing
"Sincerely" at a talent show one assembly when she was fifty
pounds younger), she didn't show it. Her face was flushed, her
eyes big moons. She and Don, and even Ratch, and even Mark
Potter from California where the bizarre future quakes up every
five minutes, were dazed by being back at the old school. "I
suddenly realize, Billy," Don said to me, "that for a whole year
I don't have a worry in the world." I think Don had left his
wife behind, but that was his business. These people all had
their own stories. One of their favorite topics all year, in fact,
was how they felt when they heard from Vic, and what they
had to break away from to be here. I could tell a lot of tales,
too, about the quickies and affairs that occurred here all year,
but I'll leave that stuff to the others to report, if they want to,
and some will. There will probably be a few stories in *True
Confessions* and *The Enquirer* about this longest high school
reunion in history.

As evening came on and cars kept arriving, Vic and I sat to
the left of the front steps in shadows. Spotlights shone up into
the maples. A waiter brought us our second bottle of
champagne. "Who the fuck is that?" Vic would whisper.
"Jesus, did you see Freddie Liston's wife?" I'd ask. We became
quietly and very happily drunk. We could hear Elvis drifting
down to us from his room directly above.

One of Vic's men barred a reporter at the front door, telling
him this was a private party, a private residence, that he was
not welcome here, and wouldn't be, and it would be best for
everyone if he left. There was a minor scene. Immediately, Vic
sent for Ellen. She found us in the shadows. "Ellen," he said, "I
want a big goddamned fence up around this whole place,
gates, guardhouse, the whole fucking works again." We'd

spoken about this at a meeting but had decided for the time being it wouldn't be necessary. We should both have known better. Three of Vic's men escorted the reporter out to New York Avenue. "No problem, Vic," Ellen said. Inside a week, the fence was up, put up by the same outfit that had done similar jobs for Vic elsewhere.

Pete Axel, a retired cop from Nassau County, came looking for us. Pete, our teammate, bench-warmer in basketball but our best chucker in baseball. When we spoke to him, shook his hand, put our arms around his shoulders, Vic and I knew that all this was right. As these friends and strangers had arrived, I'd heard a couple of remarks not "in the spirit" of the contract, remarks I hoped Vic hadn't heard, but Pete was overjoyed, teary-eyed, said he and his wife, Louise, Class of '59, loved their room, couldn't believe all this, wouldn't be able to sleep, that this was the best day of their lives. He hugged and thanked Vic, went to find Louise, who kissed us both and pulled Vic into about ten steps of a lindy right there, spilling Vic's champagne on both of them. "Come and see our room, come and see our room," she bubbled, as though Vic and I had just arrived here ourselves. Pete was even sensitive enough to pull Louise away and get lost. After all, thirty years *had* gone by, and Vic was not the exact Vic they'd once known.

Vic picked out Margo when she arrived. She looked around, probably for him, but he didn't go to her, and she disappeared into the building. He'd left a note on her bed, he said.

The vans and cars and Vic's airport limousines kept coming. It got to be too cool to sit outside. Vic and I had so much adrenaline and nervous energy and alcohol pumping in us that we went down to the gym and began to shoot some baskets. Pete found us there, and Pete had found Charlie Wright and Walt Dodd. Vic told them there were sneakers in the equipment room. They came back out to the court, and the five of us started screwing around. Some folks looked down on us from the second-floor balcony. A waiter stood at midcourt with champagne. People began to surround the floor, and other players joined us. A silly little pep rally gathered around us. I felt foolish and wonderful. I think it's important to make an ass of yourself periodically, but I heard myself laughing too loud, and worried about myself, so I calmed down, as I know how to do. And later, when I returned the ball to the equipment room, I stood in the semidark by myself for a few minutes.

At midnight there was a get-reacquainted party upstairs in one of the big lounges between the music rooms. I'm not good at meeting people I haven't seen in thirty years, but I did the best I could. Ellen helped by staying close to me. We spoke to Margo for a few minutes. She was wearing a simple combination of jeans and gray silk blouse, but she made most of the other women there look as though they'd just come in from spreading manure and milking cows. She was friendly but serious as she shook hands with the men and kissed the women who had been her friends.

I kept catching myself shaking my head—this couldn't all be happening.

Vic moved around, hugging folks, looking them straight in their eyes, welcoming them to his heaven. If he was self-conscious, he didn't seem to be. Now that he had committed himself to this, now that it had become real, he'd put behind himself, it seemed, all traces of nervousness or fright. A waiter stayed at his elbow with a silver tray of champagne that another waiter kept replenishing as Vic pressed the bubbly on everybody. Do I remember his meeting with Margo that evening? I can't quite see them together, can't see him offering her a glass of champagne. But Ellen told me a few weeks later that Jo Wagner had told her she'd gone down to the pool at four in the morning after that party and had seen Vic and Margo standing there, holding hands, talking, looking down into the water.

There was no music during the party. At first I thought there should have been, but it was right that there wasn't any—we'd have gotten the bends. And maybe it would have seemed as though we were forcing things, straining to become kids again.

Ellen and I may have been the first to leave. We were a couple now, everyone had seen. We held hands as we left the lounge. We walked down the dark hall to Ellen's room where we lay awake another hour or two, talking the day over, listening to hall echoes of doors closing, people saying good night, good night.

18

It's another September now. It seems cold down here at my station tonight. Maybe the central air conditioning is set too low. I've got a little arthritis in my left shoulder. I don't feel much like writing. Maybe I'll ask Vic if he wants to go for a drive or a walk. He's been listening to Alan Freed's "Memory Lane" album in the Ballad Room. Sometimes, only sometimes, I think that you'd think he'd get sick of some of those songs, but then I myself hear The Flamingos' "I'll Be Home," or Robert & Johnny's "We Belong Together," and I know better.

I haven't mentioned that during the time of the restoration of this place, Vic bought the old schoolhouse in Smithtown where Walt Whitman had once taught. He knocked down a couple of small businesses around it, tore up some asphalt, and made it a place the town could be proud of. Though I've not read it since, I've never forgotten the day we read Walt's poem "Crossing Brooklyn Ferry" in Skolsky's class. Walt said he was there with me, in a shining circle of water, and he was. After that, I often

sensed someone at the ponds with me, someone who had always
been there, and would be.

Also, around the time his lawyers were clearing zoning
variances for this building so we could all live in it, eat in it,
and have a bar in it, Vic donated a few million dollars to the
Town of Smithtown for its parks and recreation programs. He
turned down Kiwanis, Masons, Daughters of the Revolution,
Lions, Chamber of Commerce, and other dinners, but did stop
in briefly at the mayor's office for a key to the city. His picture
appeared on the front pages of *The Smithtown Messenger* and *The
Smithtown Star.* There was a feature in *Newsday.* A little
publicity, he said, a *little,* can sometimes take the edge off
people's curiosity, and maybe the residents would be more
inclined to leave us alone over here. A lot of publicity, he said,
and you might as well set up shop next to the statue of George
M. Cohan in Times Square.

The album just finished up, Jesse Belvin's "Goodnight My
Love," and Vic has gone back to his room. I'll leave him
alone. It's still only been a few months since our diaspora. I still
feel underwater myself. And maybe, in some ways, we've both
aged thirty years in these last months.

We were on a segment of *60 Minutes* this past Sunday. "What
was it that happened here?" Morley Safer asked the audience
as he stood outside the front gate, the school looming behind
him. "And how was it that what did happen here touched the
imaginations of so many Americans, young and old?" Half the
story was a biography of Vic, and half a mini-tour of the
building. After pressure from CBS, and after checking with Vic,
Ellen thought it best to let the film crew in. This was back
this past May. There were also interviews with a few classmates,
but the dolts CBS found were so incomprehensible about the
meanings of the experience, that Vic must have winced listening
to them, if he did. Vic's best friends shunned reporters, and
still do. Neither Vic, Ellen, or I submitted to interviews. But I
was proud of my brother. Maybe the best moment in the
program happened when Werner said, "I always knew I'd be

back here, somehow. Don't *you* know, Morley, that you'll be
back at your old high school some day?" The camera showed
that the urbane Safer *didn't* know this, but I bet tens of
millions out there in television land did know what Werner was
saying. He talked right through Morley to every greaser in the
country.

There had been a death threat against Vic, some jerk back
last fall saying that Vic's death would get American priorities
right, monies for bibles in motel rooms, and not for rock and
roll, but *60 Minutes* blew the threat out of proportion. Vic
deals with some such shit as that all the time.

There were photographs of Margo, the mystery woman, and
speculation about the reasons Vic had done all this. The show
ended with a shot of the full moon above the school, with The
Shirelles as background singing "Dedicated to the One I Love."

19

Our first assembly took place a few days after everyone arrived.
That evening, as I told him I would, I stopped by for Vic at
his room, and we walked downstairs together. I hoped he'd like
what I'd done with the auditorium.

He was nervous. For one thing, Ellen had asked him if he
wanted to say anything to the group—he said he guessed he
probably should. For another, now that his ideas had so visibly
affected so many people, had pulled them out of their own
time and space, he had second and tenth thoughts. Was any of
this his business? What was he doing here? Who the fuck

were all these people? Months later he told me that on that first day as we were walking to the auditorium he kept seeing himself at his desk in Ithaca, at Cornell, working something out on his computer, absorbed, fulfilled, by himself but too busy to be lonely.

The auditorium takes up the center of the building on the first and second floors. As we entered, evening light was streaming softly in through the same translucent windows that were in this space when we were in school. Now, instead of orderly ranks of seats front to back, easy chairs, recliners, were arranged in three concentric circles at the center of the auditorium. The inner circle had thirty chairs, the second forty-five, the third sixty-five, all in a mixture of soft beiges, browns, maroons, and grays against the background of a dark blue carpet. The second row was raised slightly above the first, the third row above the second. At the center, a circle of hardwood stage.

We were among the last to enter. Ellen had saved seats for us in the inner circle. She and I had planned the program.

Some folks clapped when Vic came in. We sat down in the dim light.

Curtains closed across the auditorium windows. I had my fingers crossed. I leaned back in my recliner, and told Vic to lean back. The whole assembly was watching Vic, and leaned back when he did.

A dome became visible above us, the blue-black vault of heaven, stars in the far reaches of space.

A minute or three of complete silence under stars, audible silence during which all those around us must have been swirling down into themselves, into this long-awaited day. I took deep breaths, thought of those around me, the thousands of cumulative years we'd been apart.

My projector rose through the floor of the stage. It looked like a mine, as planetarium projectors do. Each nozzle held a star, I thought.

The dome of heaven became the September evening sky now,

the stars seeming far distant. A low sound of wind, a meteor
shower rushing upon us, then stillness as the galaxy rotated
slowly above us. I suddenly felt so alone there in the black,
star-pointed sublime that I reached for Ellen's hand, and put my
arm around Vic's shoulders.

Music began, very low, from all around us, a few guitar
chords, then Elvis. I knew then, as maybe I hadn't completely
known before, that I still missed that poor fated bastard, still
loved him. With me, at least, he was still alive. As only he
could do it, he began singing "How Great Thou Art." I could
hear sobbing in the darkness around me, could see friends
across and to the sides of me touch handkerchiefs to their faces.

Vic wanted to say something to me, but could hardly speak.

When Elvis finished, the sobbing in the auditorium was louder.
Vic cupped my face in his hands. He said "Thank you, Billy,"
then composed himself, reached for Ellen's hand, kissed it. As I
remember, Margo was to his left. He must have turned to her.
I don't remember how she took all this. I can't remember for
sure, in fact, if she was there. She wasn't on my mind, as she
is now.

I'd taken a chance having the auditorium torn up and
redesigned. But I'd been right. Vic told me later that we had to
of course take into account the places we've been in thirty years,
the people we've become. Some of our classmates had arrived at
school dressed in the garb of the '50s—they were probably afraid
of appearing not to be in "the right spirit," afraid of jeopardizing
this miraculous windfall. But by the next day the pegged pants,
chinos, long skirts, and pink angora sweaters had been packed
away, at least until one of the sock hops we had. I'd been right
to rip out the old seats in the auditorium.

The night sky turned above us. Our solar system came into
view, then our earth in the distance, then our eyes veered toward
our earth's single moon as it grew brighter, as it became the single
source of light in the auditorium.

The projector turned over on itself and descended. All but a
small circle in the stage floor closed, but the moon hung above

us, its beams lighting the center of the stage where a podium appeared.

We sat up in our recliners. Katherine Kirk stepped onto the stage. She was/is president of our class. Katie, prim and proper in a gray suit, had never married, was a teacher in Delaware. When I'd spoken to her a few days before, she'd told me that she was on sabbatical. She said it in what seemed to me to be a condescending way, as though she had consented to join us here only because she had taken the year off from teaching, and could work on her English textbook here as well as she could in Delaware. I said very little. She'd spoken to me as though I were one of her pupils, a bit dense and callow, which I probably am. She'd spoken to me though as though I were the same person I was in high school, and only she had changed. But I have some hard miles on me, and these mean something, maybe more than subordinate conjunctions.

But even severe Katie had been moved by my planetarium effects and by Elvis's voice. As she and her podium turned very slowly, she began to speak.

"I've been asked to say a few words," she said, "a few words of welcome. As President of the Class of 1957 . . ." And then her voice trailed off as she abandoned her prepared speech. For a full revolution, she said nothing, then began again. "I'm thankful to be here among you. Am I truly alive? . . . Am I dreaming? . . . I know many of you must be asking yourselves the same questions. . . . I've thought about you so often. . . . I've seen us in these halls so often—I would have been embarrassed to admit just how often—and the odd thing is that I've pictured us not in our youthful bodies and faces but as we are now. . . ."

She recited part of a poem, I think, but I can't remember for sure. She began to whisper, but the acoustics were as good here as in a recording booth. "Dear ones, I love you all. May we be happy here in Vic's moonlight. May this moon light our way forever, on this earth and after."

"Katie, we love you, too," said a breaking voice from the third-row blackness.

Katie continued. "I want to say the names of those members of our class taken from us before our own time by illness, accident, and war.... We pledge to live for them, to keep them in our hearts during our stay here...."

As Katie said their names, the yearbook faces of our old friends appeared one by one in the cosmos above us. One faded from view as the next appeared.

"Manny Dounias ... Bob Latchen ... Gus Liparato ... Ronnie Martinson ... Phil Orlovsky ... Richie Paland ... Betty Zoller...."

Then all seven faces appeared together. The moon diminished and then disappeared to leave the faces there. The faces formed a slowly-revolving circle, clouds passing through them. I'd chosen Lee Andrews and the Hearts for this moment, that sad song "Tear Drops," ending with what for me is one of the unforgettable moments in rhythm and blues, that last line, Lee singing "Oh if we only could start over again," with the six perfect notes that comprise that last word. I can't capture that record here, of course—ideally, you'd be listening to these songs as you read our story.

The faces of our seven classmates faded away into the clouds, and then the clouds themselves faded away.

Head bowed, Katie left the stage. It was Vic's turn. Another small circle in the stage opened, and the sky filled with stars again.

I reached for Vic's hand to reassure him. His hand was cold. As I did that day under the umbrella, I could smell the lime of Vic's deodorant.... It seemed like a long time before he walked to the podium.

He was wearing a thousand-dollar gray business suit. I thought that I'd never seen him look so handsome, and so vulnerable. Twice he tried to begin talking, but his voice wasn't there. When he did speak, he spoke much too loud and aggressively, too heartily, and it took him several phrases to settle down. After the gruff "Welcome" and the croaked "You knows," he closed his eyes, listened to something inside himself, and found his voice.

"Billy and Ellen and I have been preparing for this day for a
long time.... Thank all of you for being with us.... A year
ago Billy and I stood outside during the auction of this building
and its contents.... A dream, and now we somehow return to
where we were in thirty years of light....

"We return to renew the friendship and love many of us felt
for one another during those years.... We return amazed at
what that equation of energy we call time has made of us....
We return, simply, to be together here more than halfway
through our lives.... We return in the faith that we still matter
to one another....

"People tell me I am a rich man." The first slight laughter of
the assembly. Vic played it up: "People tell me I am a *very* rich
man." Loud, open, relieved laughter this time.

"But I haven't felt very rich. Something has been missing. I'm
not sure, even now, what it has been. In all honesty, I'm not
sure I'll find it here, not sure we'll find it here together ... but
maybe we will. Or part of it. I don't know.... I know what I
do know and what I don't know.... The summer after our senior
year I was sick.... I almost died.... Then in college ...

"Do you know what I'm trying to say? I'm not very good at
this....

"Listening to Katie, seeing and hearing her as the woman she
has become, I've been self-conscious, wondering if ...

"A couple years ago I was in Germany and saw Von Karajan
conducting the Berlin Philharmonic through two long evenings
of Beethoven symphonies. It was ... that music was very
intellectual for me. It was as though, I thought, I could write
computer programs, play the stock market by that music, even
during its most lush and romantic movements.... We each have
our own music.... Each generation ... *You* were with me....
You.... Let the others go.... We are together again.... Whatever
I am looking for, I think exists inside that music I first heard
as I became myself, grew into my emotional self. This may be
true for many of you. This *is* true for you.... People will laugh

at us, will not understand us.... What we know in our deepest
hearts...."

Was Vic connecting? I knew what he was saying, but I was
sweating, grinding my teeth. It wasn't in his words that I heard
what he was saying, though. It was in his voice, which was on
the verge of cracking. Each of his groups of words seemed as
though it would be his last. There were gaps. I've made his talk
sound more coherent, no doubt, than it was. He hadn't spoken
in complete sentences. What haunted him was that he cared so
deeply for a music of puerile lyrics and rhythms seen and heard
by true lovers of Music as simplistic, unsophisticated, trite, boring,
even morally dangerous. Roll Over, Beethoven.

Vic could look prime ministers and popes, presidents and royalty,
in the eye, unashamed, but felt like a case of arrested development
when his eyes filled with tears when he listened to The Heart
Beats sing "You're a Thousand Miles Away."

He made some more starts and stops. "But never mind all that,"
he finally said. "We'll all have time now for everything we've
always wanted to say to one another. I only meant to welcome
you here, and to say that Billy and Ellen and I only wish you
to be happy and comfortable here. If there are any problems, if
there is anything we can do for you, let us know. If you have
any suggestions, let us know. Anything you want is yours."

Vic sat down again, wiping his forehead with a silk handkerchief,
taking deep breaths.

A minute of silence, the night sky streaming above us. Then
Jerry Butler singing "For Your Precious Love." Sobbing around
us again.

After Jerry's last notes, the sky brightened enough for us to
make our way out of the auditorium. Santo & Johnny's
"Sleepwalk" played softly from the sixty speakers around us.

People were hugging, blowing their noses. In the hall, I heard
words like "incredible," "unbelievable," and even that shit word
out of the '80s, "super." But all was hushed. People milled around
wanting to catch sight of Vic.

The schedule had mentioned a post-assembly bar-opening

downstairs. We'd had the bar built into what had been two
storage rooms behind the industrial arts room.

We all made our way there for a few drinks, and then most
people carried drinks to the three music rooms upstairs. A light
buffet had been set up on candlelit tables outside the music rooms
in the hall.

Everybody wanted a piece of Vic. He was at ease again now,
and loved the attention, didn't want the night to end, absorbed
their gratitude.

Katie Kirk was going from person to person, couple to couple,
in the three music rooms. . . . Bursts of laughter as people met
one another, put faces and names together ... Dave Wicks and
Lars Svanberg, in three-piece suits, found that they were both
wearing the tie bars given to us after the championship in 1957. . . .
Ratch Casano stood in the hall outside Elvis's room, swaying
in his black motorcycle jacket, stoned, tilting a magnum of
champagne. I went to him and without saying a word took his
bottle from his hand and knocked down a long drink. He winked
at me. I was glad he was here—he was one of the car gang
from the old days, the Fonzie types who were only happy when
talking tough about dragging or chicken racing, but I think he
already shared Vic's heartbeat here in the halls of our school.

I can't remember seeing Margo either down in the bar or
upstairs.

I don't know who turned out the lights that night. I saw Ellen
to her door at about three in the morning. We were both
exhausted. I went back to my own room. I wanted to be asleep
before the sounds of night's end echoed down the hall.

20

This past July Ellen moved over to the Smithtown Hotel, but still walks over here to her office every day. She and I could have kept living here, of course, but it just somehow didn't seem like the thing to do. We felt that Vic wanted and needed to be alone.

She meets with Vic most days, and takes care of the administrative stuff that still goes on even though everybody is gone. She deals with Vic's other lives, too, and is in touch with other of his offices. Once in a while there's a high-level board meeting of some kind here, Vic's head honchos flying in from all over. Vic is holding everything together, I guess, even if he's in limbo. I have a tendency to feel useless. What am I doing? I'll find my way. I don't want a briefcase and a fucking career, but I need something. Sometimes I think I could write a real book, but this is a hell of a thing to say when I still don't even want to *read* a real book.

Ellen comes in about eight, when I'm leaving. We usually meet later on for dinner and spend most evenings together before my shift begins again.

When I was a kid I used to wade knee-deep in ponds in St. James, Ronkonkoma, Lake Grove, and Nesconset, barefoot. These were the days before the ponds were garbage dumps for beer cans and broken glass. My feet would sink into the mud through soft lily pads as I caught painted turtles and frogs, or watched sunfish scoot in and out of their nests in the sandy

spots, or stuck my fingers into the black revolving balls of
thousands of tiny just-hatched catfish. But twice over those years
I got stung or bitten by something, hard. Intense pain in the ball
of my foot. I could hardly get to shore and to my bike. But a
few days later I'd be wading in a pond again. Just a couple months
ago, skimming *A Field Guide to the Insects* in Gillman's room, I
came across a plate of the water scorpion native to Island ponds.
It's an ugly brown sticklike creature with powerful mandibles.
It can inflict painful bites on man, the book says. This must have
been what jolted me those two times.

As I knew I would since I first saw her again, I've fallen in
love with Ellen. We plan to be married, but aren't sure when.
We're in no hurry. She had only one scorpion in her life, but he
must have been close to deadly.

Vic is glad for us, and this is important to us, of course. He
said it makes him happy every time he thinks of us, which is
often.

21

By day the cafeteria looked as it had when we were in school.
By night the stucco walls were covered by wood paneling or
draperies. The linoleum floor was carpeted week by week in
different shades. The long benches and tables were replaced by
smaller tables for four or six, each elegant with tablecloth and
silver, candles and crystal and Tony's flowers. There were
surprises every evening, in decor or entertainer or both.

One evening Billy Joel was playing a piano and singing as we

walked in—he's an Islander himself, and one of only a half-
dozen young entertainers Vic has much regard for. "He's got his
roots in Jerry Lee and in E.," Vic said. Another evening Nat
King Cole's daughter was there, talking about her father, singing
her own songs as we ate. Who wasn't there at one time or
another during the year? I remember that Roy Orbison and Paul
Anka showed up the same week. McCartney and his wife, Linda,
visited us, but Paul didn't cause any more oohs and aahs than
did Fats himself, or the new Silhouettes, or even Sha Na Na,
who were asked by Vic to play it straight as they serenaded us.
They did.

One evening I saw Vic walking the hall with a woman I
thought was Yoko Ono. They were talking very quietly and
seriously. I didn't bother them. . . . One day Dick Clark was at
the school, trying to talk Vic into allowing him to tape a '50s
show here, but it was no dice. . . . One day I wandered up to
one of the third-floor lounges and saw Vic sitting in a circle of
maybe a dozen friends with Jacqueline Kennedy. Most of these
visits were not announced—Vic wanted his classmates to have
unforgettable times, but somehow at the same time he wanted to
create an easygoing, natural atmosphere here. After a time, I
think, our guests were a lot more nervous about meeting us than
we were about meeting them, as Eddie Murphy seemed to be
as he joined a few of us who were shooting baskets. We thought
nothing of it one evening when Johnny Carson showed up for
a monologue down in the bar, but he seemed as nervous as though
he were auditioning for a job.

After their gig, I remember, the McCartneys seemed to want
to hang out. I was surprised. Ellen and I showed them around.
They wanted to know about Vic and our school, and I still have
a feeling that Paul is hatching some sort of reunion plan. Nobody
bothered him and Linda in the bar, and this was an evening of
heavy snow in late November, so they stayed over, their own
bodyguard camped outside their door.

The "Killer" showed up sometime during the winter for a dance
in the gym. When he opened with "Whole Lotta Shakin' Goin'

On," that first low-toned jumble of notes, I got chills, I admit.
There were a thousand miles of dirt roads and railroad tracks
in that face of his, and his ulcers were probably raw, but he
snapped his hair back as in the old days, rolled up his sleeves,
banged out those tunes with his bejeweled fingers. He finished
with "It'll Be Me." Maybe the I.R.S. was fishing for Jerry Lee,
but Jerry Lee was hanging on Vic's fishing hook, and I'm glad
he was.

Dinner was always an event, and a place. Ellen's staff began
to get suggestions about decorations. A particular Paris bistro
or London pub or Island duck house would appear overnight as
a surprise for those who'd requested it. I don't know how all
of this was done. I seldom heard even the sound of a hammer
or saw. Money can work awfully fast and quiet.

There are two things in this world I don't care anything about,
food and fashion. Never mind the food we ate here. Three
different chefs and their staffs took turns. One had run the kitchen
on a French luxury liner. Most of the fat got fatter during their
stay here, at least at the beginning.

And never mind the fashion parade that this place often seemed
to be. People afraid to grow old dress up more and more, it
seems to me, maybe to distract the eye from the body, maybe to
lift their own spirits with young colors again. I'm not immune
to this fear. I've got my own ghosts, but I don't mind my gray
hairs. I wore jeans and a T-shirt, or a flannel shirt in winter,
or maybe a sports jacket and a pair of slacks on a Friday or
Saturday night or just whenever I felt like it.

I'll fill in some other things later, but by and large you get
the picture. Before you go to sleep tonight, think of something
you would like to do or see or hear in your old high school.
It was here. We did it, saw it, heard it.

22

I still don't know all, or even much of what began to go on between Margo and Vic. I caught on to small things here and there. I didn't really care, in fact, except that I wanted Vic to find whatever he was looking for and to find out how much of that had to do with Margo. His feelings, in the end, would be the gauge of the validity and maybe even the success of what we were doing. All this, of course, was not a scientific experiment verifiable by certain tests. The only important thing would be our sense of our own well-being, and *mine,* I knew, would depend largely on Vic's. I knew that we were trying to build something that could have fallen apart on us at any time, and if it did, it would have been far worse than if Vic had been a poor man who had lived out his life avoiding listening to the old songs because they made him nostalgic, avoiding looking at his yearbook because that led to dreams of lost friends.

If this whole thing had disintegrated, and it could have at any time, Vic would have felt himself a failure, I know. What he wanted to do, somehow, was to see whether he could redeem the world for all of us, whether he could rescue our adolescence and make it meaningful for us, even now. But he couldn't begin to pass out flyers to that effect, or run editorials in the school newspaper. It would have to be something somehow created of its own force, as though we'd been drawn into this black hole of a school and had emerged into another dimension where we knew all that we knew before, and were all that we were before,

but now also were whole selves in this new world, and would
never have to deny ourselves again. If our lives grew on the
face of a thirty-year comet—but who could ever say this or write
this in the right way?

"We have wanted to *be,* and something in the current of our
culture has stopped us from being," Vic said. "Here again we
insist on being." That was the opening of his talk at an ecumenical
service one Sunday morning in the chapel. He had that written
down, and twenty minutes later looked at that slip of paper again
and said those two sentences again, but between them he spoke
of playing basketball and baseball here at Smithtown High, referred
to a disastrous first year in college, pictured himself looking
down into gorges in Ithaca into which a friend had thrown
himself, and then spoke in tongues of lasers and the warp of
starlight, of the pop electronic density of our young, of our failing
schools, of weapons systems in the cells of amoeba, of a flower's
simultaneity in blossom time and seed time and rot time.

"We have wanted to *be,* and something in the current of our
culture has stopped us from *being.* Here, again, now, we insist
on *being.*"

23

I didn't think Vic would remember my birthday, but last night
the red light on my desk lit up, and when I walked upstairs
he was waiting for me outside his door. "Let's do it," he said.
He handed me one of those blue satin flight jackets that the
astronauts had given him, and we ascended the steps from the
third floor to the roof.

Vic pilots his own planes. We sailed his copter across the cold autumn skies to Atlantic City, set down on the roof of "Vic's," his casino, had a few drinks there, and then hit other joints to gamble.

He knew I liked poker, so he had a back-room game ready for me at "Humpty Dumpty's." Humpty himself, Big Al Mogasco who used to throw golden boys around and out of the ring, sat across from me. I dragged myself out of there, drunk but with maybe five grand in my pocket. Vic had probably told Big Al to make sure I won. I threw the dough on my bed this morning, haven't even counted it yet. If Vic slept as hard as I did today, he slept hard.

I was worried, when we flew back in the half-dark, that he wouldn't be able to find the high school roof again, but there were searchlights at the roof corners that he flicked on from inside the copter as though he were operating an automatic garage door opener, and we could see our roof from maybe twenty miles away. The sky seemed to tilt us toward the school.

He stood outside his own room as I walked the length of the hall to mine. We waved to each other before I went inside. "Another forty-seven, Billy," he yelled. "Forty-eight for you, Vic," I yelled back.

24

As I was beginning to say a week or two ago, I saw things going
on between Margo and Vic last year—Ellen and I had dinner
with them at least once a week—but never spoke to Vic about
her. I took it for granted that they were sleeping together, but
I wasn't, and still am not, sure about that. It wouldn't make any
difference, in any case. It's not as though one morning I suddenly
saw Vic with a big shit-eating grin on his face that proclaimed
to us all that he'd gotten Margo into the sack at last after thirty
years and thus his search was over, that all he'd needed, after
all, was to fuck his high school sweetheart, that we could all
now go home. Nothing like that, Morley.

They did spend time together, were a couple, were linked in
the gossip columns. Once or twice Margo seemed to disappear
for a week or more. At those times Vic was so distraught that I
knew she hadn't told him where or why she was going, or even
if she'd be back.

Margo, the mystery woman, was so photogenic—even her
silhouette on the cover of *People* was alluring. Her hair was
long and still black. She wasn't the kind of person you'd ask,
either, about whether she used a color rinse, and she certainly
wasn't the kind of person who would jokingly volunteer the
information. With that hair, with her classic profile, she looked
like the archetypal woman folk-singer of the '60s. Her favorite
colors seemed to be dark-gray and black.

Sometimes I'd think about our one night together in her parents'

Rambler. Even after all these years, that didn't lighten my mood. Sometimes I suspected she knew what I was thinking.

It's not as though Margo went out of her way to be unpleasant. She spoke a few words here and there, seemed at least sometimes to be enjoying herself, seemed quietly pleased to be with Vic, but it was as though at our table for four there in the candlelit corner under the gym balcony Ellen and Vic and I had as our guest someone who did not share our past. She seemed to want to remember nothing of high school or of her years since then.

We knew from photographs that began to show up in the media that for about ten years right after school Margo had been a model. You've probably seen that ten-second clip of her on that runway in that bolero outfit a dozen times, as I have. And we knew that for the past five years or so she'd run that boutique from which she telegraphed Vic. But if Vic, or anyone, knows much about her in the intervening years, I haven't heard. She seems to have been to Europe often, but this may be a part of her recent life.

Her beauty is severe, but girlish. She didn't smile very often, and never laughed, I think because she didn't want her dimples to appear. Somehow even when her body posture would seem to say she was relaxed, the single strand of pearls she often wore seemed to be a string of incisors.

Our classmates avoided Margo. They kept away from Vic, too, when she was with him. One evening I saw Katie approach the two of them in a corner of the Ballad Room, between songs, and saw Margo cut Katie dead by turning her body at an angle that precisely divided the Vic-Margo world from hers. Katie, I thought, you can put that one in your communications textbook.

I don't know where Margo is now. She left in June when the others left. She is the one person Vic and I never talk about, and this is how I know how important she still is to him. It's up to him to bring her up, I think, not me.

They seemed to come together last year, from the beginning, automatically, by unspoken understanding. Among our other classmates, most of their high school romances were now the subjects of jokes and tomfooleries and teasing and flirting (though some while here did try to fuck their ways back into those early infatuations), but the Margo-Vic relationship was something still being worked out. I wanted to mind my own business. If Vic needed anything from me, he'd let me know. Ellen feels the same way. God knows that I didn't write the book of love, though I've lived through it a couple of times. All last year, Vic and Margo seemed to be living somewhere between the third and fourth chapters.

25

By about mid-October of last year we'd all settled into enough of a routine so that we began to get used to our new planet, mind-boggling as it was when we stopped to think about it. During the day, there were films and lectures, activities in the gym. Some people went for walks around the grounds or into town. There were shopping trips—most of us were now, of course, richer than we'd ever been. At night, dinner and gatherings in the bar and music rooms. Several people helped old Tony rake leaves around the school, I remember. Gillman had a book-discussion group. One night we all held hands around a bonfire, had a touch-football game on the lighted field, and went inside for cider and donuts.

I tried to go to most of the presentations by our classmates. People would talk about themselves/their hobbies/their families. I wish we'd videotaped those sessions—Eddie Housman with his stamp collection, Leah Budka with her macramé demonstration,

Werner and Barbara together talking about their kids and putting themselves down like Ralph and Alice Cramden to make us laugh. John Tuttle, a Mormon from Mormon heaven in Utah itself, read us a paper on church architecture, seriously and favorably comparing some new edifice in Salt Lake City with Chartres.

When Gary Rizzo had his hour, he talked about leaving school, working in a shoe store in Stony Brook on the Island, falling in love with his Theresa, getting married, losing Theresa and their young son in an automobile accident. I was looking out the window as he spoke, into the red and yellow maples. I lost my sense of where I was. I was hearing some kind of song that wasn't playing, that didn't want to allow what Gary was saying, that didn't want anything to do with what had happened to him. Or, of course, to Elvis. But it had happened, and I couldn't stay inside that song, those leaves. I was hurt, I was hurt by something other than the last thing that was ever going to hurt me, and I was surprised. When Gary was done talking, saying "That's about all, I guess," we crowded around him, comforted him as best we could. "I'm glad I told you," he said. "Now I feel as though I'm really here with you."

I guess I want to feel as though I'm really here with *you,* too.

At night the long halls of the three floors were lit with candles that made even the lockers look like shimmering water. The only commotion, if there was any, was on the top floor or in the bar sunken in the basement. I'd walk the halls with Ellen, or alone, and pass friends, sometimes stopping to talk—we seemed always, for some reason, to talk in whispers—or sometimes just saying hi and moving along past the other wandering singles or couples. It was during those late-evening and early-morning walks that I got in touch with many of my old friends. And it was during my solo ambles down the halls, when I'd veer off to stand in a classroom by myself, or go down to the gym to stand in the center circle, or look down into the pool's water, or stand in a dark corner between sections of lockers on the second floor, or sit on a stair landing listening to a song float down from above, that I could close my eyes and feel as though, body and soul, I were part of the return and reunion Vic had hoped for. Our return was a place, yes, but a more substantial place even than this building.

Ellen and I tried to talk about this. One morning she gave me a book of tiny Zen poems she'd gotten from Gillman. The book came from her, so I looked into it and got interested. She was right to think that the book would connect with my martial arts background. Never mind that. Anyway, my favorite poem was "Coming or going,/always at home." Between candles in the halls, or sitting on the dark stairs, I'd sometimes understand the thousand-year-old poem, "Coming or going,/always at home."

Sometimes, I knew, I'd be the only one awake in the whole building. Maybe I'd sit for an hour in the auditorium, project a sky above me, and lean back, thinking about the fact that I lived on a star. Or maybe I'd put on a jacket and sit on the steps outside, watching the maples, hearing the leaves scrape along the sidewalk. One or another of Vic's men walked quietly around the building all night long, or I could have felt that it was 1956 or 1957, and I was waiting to take the bus home after a late practice, or had just gotten here and was waiting for someone before going in to a dance. Before I lost myself completely, Vic's man would be back around again.

26

Already by about mid-October the times when we became bored came along more often, and stayed longer. Most of our classmates had lives back home that they missed. The bags of mail that arrived in Ellen's office every day helped, and the dinner spectacles, and the free phone calls, and the celebrities, and the sports events that Vic imported (including an evening of heavyweight boxing matches), but sometimes, in truth, it all seemed to be too much of a good thing.

Vince Clemente missed his shack and small farm in Vermont, and his wife was so homesick that it dragged him down—he hoped Annie's blues would pass, but he wasn't sure the two of them would be able to stick it out. I asked him if he wanted me to speak with Vic. No, he wasn't worried about that, he said. He knew he and Annie could leave anytime they absolutely had to. He knew that Vic would even keep sending them the money every month.

Vince wasn't the only one. I heard Tommy Vert tell Werner that he'd like to work a shift or two at Grummann's again, for a change. Tommy's wife, Leona, spent all day knitting things for her grandkids. She was biding her time, and the Verts were of course saving all that money every month, probably renting out their house, too.

Many of our friends wanted to stay in the right spirit—they had truly come to care for Vic, had gotten past the stage of celebrity awe and money awe, knew, in their own ways, that

something complex was going on here, something that
mattered even if most of them would never be able to make any
sense of it—but there was more and more forced laughter.

Vic had ears, and knew. He wondered what he could do to
make this a home for all of us, not just a place where we
marked time. I remember that about this time I overheard him
talking to Bob Dylan on the phone, telling him thanks but no
thanks, Vic didn't want him to visit us and put on a concert
here. "You're too many different people, Bob. You don't know
who you are, don't know which decade formed your soul"—Vic
said something like this to him.

Each time an entertainer or group came in, we did lose track
of our old lives for a while, but the school became quieter and
quieter, except maybe down in the bar where a few hard
drinkers, especially Ted McLaren, embalmed themselves in
Courvosier and Jack Daniels. On some weekday evenings, there
wasn't a soul in any of the music rooms.

Then, in early November, Pete Axel died. Playing a game of
basketball after lunch, the overweight Pete had collapsed. Doc
Saunders was downstairs and attending him within a couple
minutes, but couldn't revive him. Louise later told us that Pete
had had a heart attack a few years before but hadn't listed it on
the health form because he didn't want anything to get in the
way of his year here. Even if he had, we couldn't have slowed
him down. His favorite room was the Fast Dance Room.

I'd gone back to my bed that afternoon for a nap. I heard the
ambulance siren swoon along the circular drive in front of the
school, and rushed downstairs into the group of people outside
Ellen's office. "Not Vic, not Ellen, not Werner or Barbara," I
said to myself again and again as I plunged down the stairs.

Vic and I left Louise with Ellen and raced to the hospital, Vic
himself driving a limo to Port Jefferson. He was shaking his
head, asking what the fuck we were all doing here, Billy, and
saying Pete should have been at home reading a newspaper
instead of running and jumping around a goddamned basketball

court at fifty fucking years old. We followed a police car,
caught up in the draft of its siren, doing about eighty.

Pete had been DOA. Vic and I stood by his body thinking he
would bolt upright and belch or bray his horse laugh. But
there were abrasions on his face from the resuscitator, and he
was paler than we'd ever seen him. That's the way I picture
him, even now. (I picture the King with a bloated face, eyes
closed, a wreath of flowers around his neck, white satin collar
turned up, hair a little too long.)

Louise arrived with Ellen. She had heard the news from Vic.
She clasped her hands behind Vic's neck. He rocked her as
though they were slow-dancing. I put my arms around both of
them. We swayed there in that waiting room in a slow motion
that we didn't want to end, because if it did, as it would have
to, Pete would be dead.

Other friends arrived from the school and put their arms
around us. We cried until we were cried out, and then broke
up, eased out by nurses and doctors. I remember that I again
felt the cold and selfish but very real comfort of being alive
myself. My turn's coming, I said to myself. I wondered if Pete's
spirit could see me as I stood in the hospital corridor.

Vic asked Louise to come back with us, asked her if she
would like Pete brought back to the school that evening for a
memorial service. She said yes, said Pete would have wanted it
that way, said she was so thankful to Vic for giving Pete the
months of anticipation and then these past months at school. She
said that she somehow knew this was going to happen, knew
it from the time of Ellen's first call. Pete had been so happy, she
said, had been *too* happy.

Outside, I blew breath steam into the autumn air, small
ascending souls that disappeared.

On the ride back to the school, Louise sat between Ellen and
me in the backseat. Vic and Margo were in the front, beyond
the dividing glass. Vic was on the phone, making arrangements.
Louise was shivering, beginning, now, to realize what had
happened. We pulled a blanket around her.

That evening, Pete's closed casket revolved slowly on the stage in front of us under sprays of white lilies. His coffin was cherrywood, with silver fittings. We sat in our three circles around him, holding hands. Elvis sang "That Old Rugged Cross."

Our classmate Charles Edmunds, a Lutheran pastor, and maybe Pete's closest friend thirty years before, spoke, said that we would now support Louise with our love, said that Pete, surely, could see us, now, around him.... Charles couldn't finish. I could see him beginning to lose it. It was Margo who went to the podium and helped him down.

Vic stood up, stuttered a few sentences. "I loved/love Pete," he said. "I'm so sorry.... I know Pete was happy here, being here with all of us, and this is our consolation, you know, but I'm so sorry.... Maybe ..."

We sat in silence and held hands for several minutes. Music began again, Elvis singing "Amazing Grace." Pete's coffin stopped turning. Louise went to the stage and knelt by Vic's knees, pressing in against flowers and against the coffin. Vic knelt down with her. All of us joined them there, knelt on that stage under the night sky with Pete as Elvis sang, the dead singing for the dead, the living only overhearing.

27

I didn't go back to my apartment right away this morning, but stayed until about eleven with Ellen in her office. She had time for coffee, between calls and visits from Tony, Doc, and the head security man from out at the gate. Nothing pressing.

They like being with her, seeing her every day, as I do. Tony brings her a corsage every day.

She had something to tell me. A jeweler from New York, accompanied by a security guard, had visited Vic yesterday upstairs. Margo was to visit us, Vic told her, early in December. Ellen thought Vic was going to propose to her. Maybe he already had.

I knew Ellen was thinking what I was. There was no guarantee that Margo would marry Vic, and if she didn't, Vic would be even more dissociated than he seemed to be now, and if she did, it could be that she would make him miserable. Long before this, Ellen had told me that Margo never did send that "right spirit" contract back to the school. She did, apparently, deposit the monthly checks. Not that signing that contract made any difference about anything. It was at least as silly as it was serious, of course. It was just that Margo had been different from the rest of us from the beginning of this return, leaving the school without letting anybody know where she was going, sometimes seeming to be away even when she was here.

Our only concern was Vic. Margo had never insulted either of us, had never overtly offended us in any way, but she herself didn't seem to have feelings that could be hurt, while Vic was wide-open for a wipe-out.

I can hear Vic up in the Ballad Room. He's singing along with a Jack Scott album, his deep voice blending into "My True Love" and "With Your Love." "How can I go wrong?" Jack and Vic ask. I don't think Vic has proposed yet.

28

Louise Axel didn't come back to school after Pete's death, though she was of course welcome to stay with us.

If anything, many of us, including Vic, began to work out more often, in the weight room, on the basketball court, the men beginning to play full-court games. Someone was always in the pool. The women had a daily aerobics session, moving to oldies—I saw their routine to Faye Adams' "Shake a Hand" and can still see them now, most of them seeming to me not older but better, as the saying goes. So many attractive and balanced women in our class, and theirs had been a confusing, even tortured generation. All the family and career issues, the male chauvinist and feminist issues had been battles in their own lives, and here they were. I felt—this is corny, I know—proud of them all, fond of them, wanted to embrace them as Vic said that old Walt, the spirit of this Island, wanted to embrace everyone. I wondered if I was becoming sappy in my old age.

Many of us limped down to Doc's office for whirlpool treatments or bandaging after workouts. There was a mixed volleyball match almost daily, too, afternoons, toning people up for dinner. The truth is, we were no longer bored. Because we were human, Pete's death had made us afraid, yes, but there was more to it than this. It had wised us up. The death of our friend had done something to our sense of time here.

I remember talking with Harold Molinoff and his wife during one of my two-in-the-morning auditorium visits. I'd walked

down to my usual seat in the inner circle and had sat down
without at first seeing them. They were glad to have company.
We leaned back and spoke quietly.

Harold and Angie had thought a lot about Pete. Harold, a
lawyer, had a practice in Hempstead and stayed on top of it by
phone from here at the school and by an occasional visit, but he
missed the nuts-and-bolts of it. And Angie, who drove a
school bus (two of their three children were married, and the
youngest was a senior at Ithaca College), missed those excited
and yammering kids. Here, Harold and Angie had kept more to
themselves than most of the others, had gone back to their
rooms right after dinner most nights just to read and call their
families and kill time, but Pete's death had drawn them
down to the bar for a drink and up to the area of the music
rooms for companionship now. They had as many years as the
Lord would give them for that other life, Angie said. Until
June, they wanted, now, to get to be as close as they could to
their classmates. They'd gotten to be dear friends with Louis
Soskin, a bachelor who had dated Angie in high school. They
and Louis had coffee almost every day with Miss Koch, too,
their old Latin teacher, and with Katie—Katie and Louis had
been seeing each other, Angie said, winking at me.

When Margo skipped dinner, Vic would join people at
different tables. Just the night before, Harold said, he and
Angie had had dinner with Vic, their first real chance to talk
with him, as this was their first real chance to talk with me.
"Billy, it's all in his voice, you know," Harold said. "It's not
anything he says. He was talking about his casino, then about
a race horse—I'd told him Angie and I had vacationed at a
dude ranch in Virginia once—but all the while, we knew, he
was thinking about that very moment, about being here with us
in this school again. Angie and I have discussed this. There's
always something behind whatever he's talking about, something
that lets us know we're *here* where we are supposed to be."

Angie wondered if Vic had ever taken up this thing they call
TM, transcendental meditation. No, I told her, so far as I

knew, Vic didn't meditate, at least not in any formal way. I
thought of Elvis. Of all the futile . . .

Yes, Vic was thinking about what Harold said he was, but he
was thinking about this by thinking about Margo up in her
room or wherever she was. She was the embodiment for Vic of
what we were doing here. When she missed dinner, when she
was unhappy, which she seemed most of the time to be, Vic was
out-of-sync. He could be talking to one of us, and seem to be
with us, when he wasn't, except by way of his concentration on
Margo.

On our way out of the auditorium I showed Angie where to
shut off the dome projector. The stars disappeared with a
click.

We went down to the bar for a glass of champagne—maybe
twenty people were still there. I kissed Angie good night, then
shook Harold's hand. As I did, I looked into his eyes, actually
looked at Harold for the first time since I'd seen him again in
September. No, I looked at him for the first time ever. From
that point on, I told myself, I would *see* my old friends when I
spoke with them. I didn't have time anymore, I thought to
myself, to be staring at the ground and shuffling my feet. I
read somewhere once that a wise and humble man learned to
look at the ground when he walked through life, but I'd guess
that a wise and humble man would want to keep learning, and
there was a lot to learn just looking into people's eyes. I hate
the businessman's glad handshake and eye contact learned at
some seminar, but I could begin to look into my friends' eyes
when we spoke, instead of being some kind of furtive skulker.
This would connect with living in the present, too.

I remember that just before I went to bed that night, walking
the length of the hall on the third floor, I thought I'd passed a
ghost. But it was only Phil, hovering outside the Ballad Room,
weaving and jangling his jewelry to the sound of The Teddy
Bears doing "To Know Him Is to Love Him."

29

Thanksgiving dinner last year ... A buffet-style smorgasbord
was set up, and because people were free to invite their
families—Ellen had to draw the line somewhere, so couples
were allowed to invite eight guests and single people five—the
gym also became a second dining hall. There were dozens of
huge turkeys waiting for the carving at center tables, bowls of
shrimp, pecan and pumpkin and custard pies. Excited talk
throughout the building, many grandkids, families being
shown around the place, Vic his old excited self for a change.
There was an evening planetarium show in the auditorium,
programmed by the staff of the Hayden. After that, a dance in
the gym, which had been cleared and decorated. Small log
cabins had been built against walls of pine boughs. I half
expected to see groups of colonists, or maybe Bull Smith
himself would round a corner on Whisper.

At midnight and later, I sat with Ellen in her office. The
year's first snow was sifting down as we watched our
schoolmates say good-by out front to family and visiting friends.
Car doors closed beyond the steps. But these were not sad
partings. Our friends were still turned on as they came back into
the building and headed down for nightcaps or up to the
music rooms.

When Ellen and I wandered upstairs later, we saw that no
one was in the Ballad Room or even in Elvis's room. The Fast
Dance Room was mobbed, Chuck Berry and Buddy Holly were

turned up louder than I'd ever heard them. Someone turned
up The Cadillacs, while they were singing "Speedo," even
louder. We winced and laughed under the decibel-pressure. It
didn't even bother me when someone twice in a row blasted the
one tune I was truly sick of: may Bill Haley and his Comets
rest in peace, but I never want to hear "Rock Around the
Clock" again. I prefer quiet torture, Chinese water torture, to
all that noise. I'm a sucker for any sappy ballad, but "Hound
Dog" rock has always worn thin for me fast.

Ellen and I went for a walk in the snow. Smithtown was
already decorated for Christmas, reindeer and elves perched
above the streetlamps. The weeks were going by faster than we
wanted them to, and our classmates, we knew, now felt the
same way.

I don't think either one of us slept much that night. We lay
in the loft bed in her room watching the snow, trillions of
intricate hexagons, fall through the bare trees.

30

The school is so quiet tonight that I got spooked a few hours
ago, and went down to make some noise and shoot some
baskets. But the hollow sound of the ball echoing in the gym
didn't help much. I generally like to be alone, but on nights
like this the gym is filled with ghosts, and I could use a record of
crowd noises as I shoot.

I went to the library and picked up a little book—actually, it
seemed as though I was holding it before I saw it or reached

for it—called *Zen in the Art of Archery,* by Eugen Herrigel. I
read it through in a couple hours, but need to read it again.
Herrigel was a German who went to Japan to study archery
with a master, while his wife studied the art of flower
arrangement. What the archer must aim for, says Herrigel's Zen
master, is himself. Hitting the target at the center will be
incidental to the discipline itself. At first, in learning to draw the
bow easily, the author made good progress, but then ran
against a wall, and spent months trying to learn to release the
arrow without doing it deliberately. He tried everything, but
there seemed no way for him to will a pure release into being.
Once, he even tried a trick, and his relationship with the
master was almost terminated. His ego and anxiety were
constantly in the way as he tried to let the arrow let go of
itself. The book gave me the words for many of the things I
know. You can't shoot a basketball, or throw a kick, by
thinking about it. You have to do it for its own sake. You have
to do it without doing it. You have to do it as part of a circle,
a whole. Releasing a shot, or a kick, comes from somewhere
beyond us, in its own time.

No pun intended on the word "release," but while writing
this I just thought of how unselfconsciously some of our
favorite old songs came into being—this was before the
manipulators, characters with degrees in adolescent psychology,
took over. Remember the true story of how Elvis came up with
"That's All Right"? Between taping sessions he just started
letting loose and acting like a jerk, jumping around and giving
in to a little lyric he'd found in his head. The other players
joined in, in the right spirit. One of my favorite records was the
result. And there's a story about the first time Roy Orbison
heard that record: he didn't understand it, it scared him, and he
had to play the flip side, the traditional "Blue Moon of
Kentucky," to reassure himself. And the next time you get the
chance, listen closely to Fats' "Blueberry Hill." Right in the
middle the sound sags and warps, slows down, but who cared if
the production was imperfect? The natural sound of the thing

caught us where we lived. Those voices didn't have to be
filtered and echoed through a hundred sound chambers before
we heard them. I heard the Ramones complain about Phil
Spector once, in fact. They got antsy and then went nuts when
Phil spent hours and hours trying to get one fucking opening
chord right. This ain't the way a song gets sung, in the end.
I'm not an educated man, but I know that much. My hand can
move through boards of its own volition, of my body's
volition, of my soul's body's volition. But with just my brain
talking to my hand, I can't bust a balsam beam. To put it
another way, if you spend your life trying to perfect an orgasm,
you'll never know what it is to make love.

At the end of the little Zen book, Herrigel's master shoots out
a candle in the dark from maybe fifty yards away. The master
seemed only to be half looking. I walked down the hall to
where Eddie Rogas used to sit, and placed a candle on his
desk. I lit it and walked back here to my desk, looking down
the hall to the candlelight, squinting at it, imagining loosing
an arrow toward it. Then I closed my eyes, and I could still see
the candle. At least there was a source of light there at the end
of the corridor and in the center of my brain. Even if I don't
know what the mysterious "it" is that must release the arrow,
as Herrigel didn't know, as maybe the Master didn't know and
didn't need to know, I know the "it" is there. Without it, I
think, these past two years would never have happened.

All along, Vic has sensed all this. We have been lofting
ourselves through the dark. Ideally, we would have no target
in mind except ourselves. At the ends of the halls in our old
high school building, some sort of eastern Einsteinian curve
occurs, time and ourselves returning to where we have always
been. Does this make any sense? What we did here last year,
what I am doing here now, is either down the center of what
the Zen experience is all about—those tiny poems Ellen gave
me freeze nature so that we can actually see it for an instant,
but this doesn't mean that nature is not constant flux—or is so
far from the mark that I've had my back turned to the candle

all my life. And how to know? I do know that I'm glad I'm here, here now. Ellen has come home to me from where we always were. If I only had the years to do over again—I'd learn enough about all this so that I'd be solid enough in my own being to be able to save someone I love.

From the beginning when Vic and I stood under his umbrella at the auction, Vic trusted. This is the thing. He didn't know what would happen, didn't have a particular target in mind. Aiming for himself (though he wouldn't think about it in this way), trusting his own emotions, he went ahead. This is not good *business,* of course. Vic didn't project outcomes, didn't stop himself just because he did not know what, if anything, would happen. He didn't take any polls or surveys. He knew everybody else in his class felt some of what he felt, and he hoped to tap into those feelings. If he'd tried to program the year of the return, he once told me, his computer would have replied "Insufficient Data" or "Are You Kidding?"

When Herrigel once managed to release an arrow naturally, it was an "accident." The master told him not to be proud of himself, told him to bow down to the "it" that had released the arrow, told him that since he wouldn't as a matter of course be able to repeat the perfection of that shot, he should go home and consider what had happened. The next day, of course, Herrigel's releases were forced and self-conscious again. He had to start all over again. He was no master.

The candle down at Rogas' desk has burned down, is almost out. I'm going to light one there every night to remind me of some things. Even when I'm not looking at it, and most of the time I won't be, it will be there in the iris of my tongue's eye as I write.

31

I just got back from the gym. I didn't turn on any lights. For about an hour, with my eyes closed, I lofted foul shots. The less I aimed my shots, the less my goal was to make the shots, the more they went in. I could hear the ball pass through the net, but even curiosity about whether or not my shot went in was a perversion of my motives, the master would say. The purer I was, the more likely it was that the ball would flow through the hoop—though this didn't matter, I kept telling myself. But I was still, of course, too self-conscious. I threw up some air balls. But I now have some sense of where the basket is, and it's not up there ten feet from the floor, fifteen feet away from me, in my old high school gym. . . .

I was just looking through one of Ellen's old weekly schedules to remind me of what all happened last year at about this time. I remember now the party in early December at Nick's.

We all walked from school to our old soda parlor hangout. Ellen and I were with a group of about a dozen others, throwing snowballs along the way. Piling into the place, shaking snow off our coats and stamping our feet, we laughed easily at ourselves now, at this whole thing our genie Vic was pulling off. It was already winter, and those who still missed home realized they'd be back before they knew it. Many now knew that they'd be back home before they wanted to be.

As we came in, Vic was at the door, shaking hands, kissing

the women. Some of us hadn't been down to Nick's before, as
I hadn't, though I'd glanced in a couple of times while out
walking. Everything was as I'd remembered it, the long
counter with stools, the booths, the small square of a dance
floor, the Coke pictures and Hires root beer signs. But Vic had
expanded the place a good distance out back for a stage and
about twenty more booths.

At first, it was only the old jukebox playing our old songs,
but then a curtain opened out back and the Everly Brothers
were there, opening with "Wake Up Little Susie." Some women
in the aerobics group ad-libbed one of their routines to the
song. Cokes and hamburgers, milkshakes and pizza, all around.
Then forty or fifty couples slow-dancing to "Dream." Phil and
Don seemed to be getting along okay.

I can't remember whether or not Margo was there. She wasn't
at the door with Vic when we came in, I know. Do I see them
dancing, or am I just imagining it now? I want to ask Ellen if
she remembers if Margo was there, and if so how Margo took
the whole thing.

Maybe I haven't been sympathetic enough. What if Margo
were just congenitally unable to get into touch with the
romance we were living, and had spent that night all alone in
her room at the school, or maybe wandering the halls, looking
for herself?

I remember seeing a television interview with Cary Grant,
hearing his answer when he was asked whether in the end he
felt irrelevant and stupid making so many movies with such
glitzy settings. "Is a garbage can any more real than
Buckingham Palace?" he snapped.... And I remember hearing
Katharine Hepburn say to Merv Griffin—these are her exact
words—"One doesn't always know why one's life goes to hell,
does one?"

I remember that Ellen and I slept that night at my apartment
in town. This was generally against the contract, but it was
still in the right spirit, we giggled. Under covers, we asked each
other if that place, the high school, was really over there just a

couple blocks away, or whether we'd gotten married the month
after high school, had settled here in Smithtown, and had
imagined this whole thing. Maybe we'd snap out of our amnesia,
and she'd pick up her job as a waitress in the morning, and
I'd go back to an eight-to-five burnout until my head fell off.
Maybe next summer we'd see an announcement in the local
papers about the upcoming auction of the school and its
contents, and we'd go to the auction and meet Vic Holyfield
there, and Vic would have taken the day off from his janitor's
job somewhere maybe to bid on and try to afford an eraser or
pencil from his old school. Maybe we even scared each other a
little with our retroactive fantasies.

But the next morning we got dressed in the present again,
and when we walked over to the school for breakfast, from
even two blocks away we could see Vic's helicopter on the
school roof.

32

I only got drunk once last year, and that was on the final night
of our Christmas basketball tournament. For this, everybody
was asked to dress in outfits of the '50s. There would be a sock
hop after each game.

It was a two-evening tournament, four teams. We had our
club, augmented with a couple ringers, and Ellen and her staff
had put together three other teams of players from our old A-2
league and added some ringers to them, too.

The first evening, Smithtown played against a team from the

Northport area. Bob Sherer and Bobby Wine were both back,
their high scorers in the winter of 1956–57, when we'd beaten
them by one point in a play-off game when Dave Wicks, our
worst shooter, threw up one of his two-handed off-the-forehead
jumpers in the last second and it swished. Vic and I met Bob
and Bobby at mid-court. Wilt Chamberlain was the ref that
evening, and when the five of us shook hands, Wilt's two
huge mitts covered our eight.

As we waited for Wilt to stop clowning around and throw up
the ball for the center jump, Bobby Wine told me he'd read
about this thing we had going on in Smithtown, but somehow
hadn't believed it. Cheerleaders were leading cheers for both
teams, and an '80s-style wave crested around the gym as we
talked.

After high school, Bobby had played baseball for the Phillies
and then the Expos when the league first expanded. "I've seen
some strange things, Billy, but never nothing like this," he said
to me later in the game as we looked at all the middle-aged
teenagers in the stands. "Think of it as a masquerade party,
Bobby," I said. From the stands and balcony flashbulbs were
popping off by the dozens. For some excitement, Vic had
opened the place up to the press. There must have been at
least one reporter there from every big paper in the country, and
usually three: a sports writer, a photographer, and a society
reporter. You've seen some film clips of those evenings.

We beat the Northport team easily, though Elgin Baylor, slow
and gimpy as he was, threw in about thirty. The Smithtown
Indians were 1 and 0, and could finish up an undefeated season
the next night.

Vic didn't play much in the Northport game. Coach Mularz
was there with Red Auerbach as his assistant, but we substituted
ourselves when we felt like it, and Vic felt like sitting out
most of the game. He didn't start, in fact, but from the time we
came out in our red-and-white warmup outfits, whenever Vic
made a basket or clowned around, the crowd roared. He was
the star. When he came in to start the second eight-minute

quarter, all the other nine players on the floor hoisted him up
and carried him over to a spot along the foul lane. We told
him to stay there and stay out of trouble. When he hit his first
shot, a banker from the right side, a hundred of Tony
Piccione's carnations rained down around him. Sam Jones, *the*
bank shooter of all time, gave Vic a low five, and a waiter
wearing a tuxedo and sneakers came out with a glass of
champagne for Vic—this had been Ellen's idea. She'd hoped
Vic would make at least one shot. Vic raised the glass, toasted
the crowd, and drained the champagne. You've seen that
photograph.

When I took a good look at the Smithtown cheerleaders for
the first time—Lynn Reddinger, Bobbi Cohen, Alice Wagner,
Pat Berryman, and the rest—I was amazed to see Margo. She'd
been a cheerleader, of course, but I hadn't expected to see her
sharing in all the foolishness. From fifty feet away, she looked
like the girl she'd been—knee socks, short pleated skirt, bulky
sweater, hair in a ponytail. I remember seeing her teeth, so
maybe she even smiled once. I watched Vic look over at her
several times as though saying, "Didn't I tell you?" or "Have
some fun, Margo, whatever we're doing," or "I know I'm
making an ass of myself, but I've got nothing better to do
tonight, so what the hell." The women had been practicing,
apparently, and snapped off some good routines. Margo had
Vic's name for the team cheer at half time, yelling "Vic, Vic,
he's our man," Ellen later told me. I was in the bar with the
other ballplayers during the half. Anyway, Margo was trying
hard, at least. I had to give her that.

Before our game with Northport, Patchogue had beaten
Hauppauge, despite Senator Bill Bradley's forty, so we played
Patchogue the second night. They had the Tedaldi twins
back—both looked like they'd been working construction all
their lives, looked meaner and leaner than they had in high
school. They had Marques Haines, the great Globetrotter
dribbler, and Jerry West. They had old Sweetwater Clifton on
the bench. But I haven't mentioned our own ringers. Vic and I

started the Patchogue game along with last-shot Wicks, Lars
Svanberg, and Peppy Callahan from our old team, but when
ringer subs came on for both teams, Bob Cousy and Tommy
Heinsohn came in for us. I'd loved Heinsohn since he'd played
at Holy Cross, before going on to the Celtics. He was heavy
now, but graceful, and boxed out one or both the Tedaldi
twins underneath as though they were standing in cement.
Cousy, in the most memorable play of the tournament,
dribbled to the foul line on a three-on-one fast break, jumped,
turned around in the air, and flipped a perfect lead pass from
over his left shoulder to Vic in the right lane for a lay-up.
That's the shot that you saw Vic make on the cover of *Time.*

All of us had to sit out often, but we skipped the half-time
bar that second night and played seriously. A couple of us old
Indians, myself included, are better ballplayers now than we
were in high school. I was such a skinny kid, painfully skinny,
six foot four and maybe 130 pounds. I'm 205 now, and have a
jump shot that I didn't have back in those days when you saw
as many two-handed set shots as you did jumpers. Svanberg was
the best jump-shooter in the league, and carried us to the
championship. (At that time on the Island, by the way, it was
Carl Yazstremski, playing over in Bridgehampton, who was
averaging about forty-five points a game, setting all kinds of
records. If Yaz had been six inches taller, he'd have played for
the Knicks or Celtics, maybe, instead of the Red Sox.)

Vic, too, is in good shape, not marathon shape but maybe
occasional sprint shape. That night against Patchogue it was as
though two well-matched over-forty town teams were playing.
No, it was better than that. The pros still shone. I choked up
when West hit two long shots, shots that clunked hard against
the back of the rim as they buried themselves, as his shots
always had. They weren't town-team shots.

Red Auerbach lit up one of his cigars. I think Smithtown
won. It didn't matter. At the end of the game, Bill Russell, the
ref that night, grabbed Vic and the senator and held their hands
high. Vic waved for all the players from the four teams to join

them at center court. He picked up a mike and thanked the
cheerleaders. He asked the spectators to applaud themselves.
He said something like if we could play back the sounds
absorbed by the wood of these old walls, we would hear
ourselves again as we once were, and now the sounds of these
two evenings would join those sounds from those other years,
and all would be one, at once, so bless us. He said that there
was a cyclic light in this gym that would be here in this space
on the planet even after this brick building in its now
non-Euclidian geometry had disappeared. The truth is that no
one knew what the hell he was saying, but it didn't matter. Vic
had done it. Because of him, I was standing on the same court
with some of the men I'd grown up with. I was standing on the
same court with other men that I'd lived inside when I
watched them on television. I now called the old pros by their
first names. Each evening a few of my shots had gone in, and
the men had slapped me on the ass and said, "Good hit" or
"Again." And all those on my high school team were in fact
still alive. Through luck and God's grace we'd grown old
together, and not without a certain dignity that this silly
evening had even, somehow, managed to highlight, I think.
Maybe not the least of Vic's gifts was that he'd given us our
sense of humor back. Who says that when we're forty or fifty or
sixty we have to act as though we'd been born as bureaucrats
and stockbrokers?

Vic asked Ellen to come out with the gifts for the players.
Each received a lucite cube in which floated a mint ten-dollar
U.S. gold piece. I have mine in front of me on this desk as I
write, a quietly dignified Indian incised on its face.

I looked down at the court and closed my eyes. . . .

Soon the lights went down, Danny and the Juniors came on
over the speakers, and the sock hop began. I rushed my
shower to get back out there with Ellen.

Later, I stayed at the bar even after almost all the others had
gone up to the music rooms or to bed. I was exhausted, and so

exhilarated that even the obnoxious McLaren, who had lectured
Bill Bradley all night, couldn't bother me.

Ellen kissed me good night, but knew enough to leave me
there in my daffy happiness and go up to bed. I don't know
how I eventually got up to my room. I know that I suffered
plenty the next day, couldn't eat much but toast and tea. But
the Smithtown Indians were champions again and still, and Doc
Saunders, in his infinite generosity, gave me a couple of his
hangover placebos and a lecture.

33

Margo is in town, though I haven't seen her here at the school
yet. Last night Vic told me only that he and Margo had some
things to work out.

"She's not a happy woman, Billy," he said. "I wish I could
change that." Half the time, to me, the Vic-Margo merry-go-
round is about as interesting as a cookbook, but there was
anguish in his voice. We feel responsible, like it or not, for the
happiness or unhappiness of those we love.

There are things I've wanted to ask him, but I know better.
Really, it's none of my business except that Vic is not centered
this year, is scattered and restless, is still looking for something.
I have the feeling that last year would have been enough for
him, magical and fulfilling, if only Margo had snapped out of
her funk into some kind of contentment, but now another
indecisive year has been going by for Vic. And I know, too, that
Ellen and I would have even more than we have now—and

now we have each other and a future, and this is more than we
could have imagined after our other experiences—if only Vic
were happier. This is not a matter of Vic's finding himself. In
some ways, he did find himself (whatever that means), has the
confidence to be himself now, has integrated his selves
now, knows where he lives now (and I don't mean in this
building), but he can't seem to find Margo. She is the displaced
person, and because she is, the other three of us never quite
have our feet on the ground. I hope the jeweler went home with
a fifty-carat smile on his face. I hope Vic doesn't wind up, in
the end, slipping a rejected diamond to some waitress for a tip.

Ellen said that she spoke with Katie about Margo. "It's
simple," Katie had said. "She's a bitch."

I can't anticipate what might happen. So far, to me and to
Ellen, the situation seems impossible. If there's a worldly thing
that could make Margo happy, Vic hasn't found what it is. If
Margo doesn't herself know why she seems so often to be a
semi-depressive, Vic is going to have to get lucky to help her.
Maybe I should do a few lines of coke with Margo, and try to
get her to talk. Maybe I should buy an old Rambler and ask her
for a date and try to exorcise any lingering guilt between us.
Maybe, seriously, I should talk to Doc about her. No.

"You know, Billy," Vic said, "I do love her, but don't know
what to do about her. She wasn't always so quiet, was she?
She wasn't quiet in high school, at least. It's not something
simple, not as though she's worried that I care for her only
because I'm trying to get my youth back. I don't think she
thinks I'm crazy, or will kill both of us in the helicopter, you
know, or will buy Graceland and force her to live in a room
filled with E's godawful gaudy last Las Vegas outfits."

Nutty things occurred to me: Margo still loved me and had
borne our child after our one fuck; Margo was married to
someone already; Margo was a lesbian; Margo was not Margo,
was an impostor who had killed the real Margo and now
could speak very little because she might give herself away;

Margo was having an affair with gossamer Phil Spector under our noses all last year. Enough nonsense.

Down at the end of the hall, my target-candle is flowing. I don't think I could hit it with a shotgun tonight.

34

A couple days before Christmas last year, an ice storm hit the Island. Power was out all over. Here at the school, thanks to Vic's foresight, we were on our own generators.

Then, Christmas eve, a snowstorm. LaGuardia and Kennedy airports in the city were closed down, as well as MacArthur in Islip, out here on the Island. Bus and train schedules were canceled, the Expressway and other highways buried. Even when they left the town garages, there was no place for snowplows to push the stuff. Thick ice under heavy snow.

We were isolated at the school. There would be no Christmas visitors. Even the phone lines were out. But it was cozy here, as warm in the building as it had ever been, though we all wore our thickest sweaters anyway. We sipped hot rum toddies all day, and looked out at the weather. The snow must have drifted six feet deep in front of the school. Not a dent in the snow until the guards at the gate plowed a path in case of an emergency, though it would have taken a tank to get to a hospital from here. I wouldn't have been surprised, of course, if it turned out that Vic did have an old Sherman in one of the garages.

Everybody up and around, not wanting to be alone.

Everybody early for lunch. Then a call went out for cooks,
and for workers to decorate the cafeteria. All food and props
were on hand, but the kitchen and construction crews couldn't
get here. We all got together under Vic's direction, some in the
kitchen and some in the cafeteria, to set the place up. We felt
like kids again. More laughs than I can ever remember. Then
we left to change for dinner, and came back.

The gym seemed to have become a hill in Bethlehem, stars
above us, and the one Christ star pulsing brighter than the
others. We sat on cushions around flat-topped boulders, eating
Long Island duckling, serving ourselves, drinking red wine.
The wise men knelt in a crèche under the balcony. In the
candlelight of the gym, in the glow of wine, in the soft
background music of Elvis singing carols, in the knowledge that
snow was deepening around us, it seemed to me to be a holy
evening. Vic had made room at the inn for us.

Later, we watched *White Christmas* in the theater, exchanged
gifts, said good night to one another with eggnog toasts. Vic
gave me several cassettes. I think I know what they are, though
I haven't had a chance to listen to them yet. Well, we do what
we want to, in the end. Maybe I'm just not ready yet, or I'm
saving them for a time when I might need them. Or
something.

That night, Ellen and I fell asleep in each other's arms, but
she soon nudged me awake. "Listen," she said.

The school had gone quietly to sleep when we'd gone to bed.
Now we could hear music again.

We put on our bathrobes and slippers, and walked into the
hall, as did others. The word went around that an assembly
service would begin in a few minutes. Ellen didn't know
anything about this. Vic was up to something.

Ellen and I helped tap on the doors of any of our friends who
were still sleeping. The halls were lit softly with blue
Christmas lights. When we passed any window to the outside,
we saw that it was still snowing. Big, shadowy flakes.

Vic and Margo were already in their seats in the auditorium

when Ellen and I sat down next to them. Vic was in his
bathrobe, but Margo was dressed in her jeans and a bulky
sweater. She strained to smile for Ellen and me. Our
classmates filled in around us, almost all in their robes.

A Christmas tree, a Colorado blue spruce that must have been
twenty feet high, turned slowly on the stage. Its blue-green
fragrance filled the darkness. It, too, was decorated with only
blue lights, a bluer star on its crown. There were blue stars in
the dome above us, one bluest star rising in the east.

I was holding both Ellen's hands in mine. I closed my eyes
and said a childhood prayer that I'd not thought of for as long
as I could remember: "I thank Thee my heavenly Father that
Thou hast kept us this day, and I pray Thee that Thou wilt
graciously keep us this night, for into Thy hands we commend
ourselves, our bodies, our souls, and all things." I was
surprised the prayer was still with me.

Had I ever heard Elvis sing "Ave Maria" before? I don't
think so. I haven't heard it since. Did I hear it that night,
Schubert's beautiful and yearning song of love for the mother of
Jesus sung by the truckdriver from Tupelo, Mississippi, that
lost soul? You know that Elvis loved his mother as much as
Schubert loved Mary. I wondered if others were thinking
about this as Elvis sang.

McLaren was bawling like a baby somewhere across the way.
I wasn't much better. I was sobbing, Ellen comforting me, Vic
patting me on the back, people behind me leaning forward in
the darkness to touch me. Across the room, through the three
circles, our friends looked into one another's eyes and said "I
love you, dear friend, I love you and always will," or didn't
have to say anything but just embraced one another back
through the thirty years all the way to now.

The tree went dark, descended. Silence, then the *whoosh* of a
star shower above us, but the messiah star steadfastly shining
blue, slowly coming closer, finally bursting and scattering in a
shower of sparks.

The blue tree rose from below the stage again.

Vic drew Margo up to the tree, and asked us all to join hands
with them. We all came forward around the tree. There was a
minute's silent prayer. Then Elvis sang "O Holy Night." We
had all been in this room for two thousand years, I thought.
Maybe we had always been here. Maybe this was the night that
Elvis himself would join us here. My old friend began singing
"I'll Be Home for Christmas."

This time when Elvis was done singing, stage lights came on,
and Vic said, "Merry Christmas, Merry Christmas."

"Merry Christmas, Vic," McLaren bellowed from across the
way, shaking the whole tree as he lurched around it to reach
Vic. We all needed to laugh. Vic hugged McLaren and asked
him down to the bar for a nightcap, on the off chance that
McLaren ever imbibed.

"Vic, I will drink no more," McLaren said solemnly and
fervently as he walked down the blue-lit hall with Vic. "But I
will drink no less," he shouted.

Walking behind them, I had Ellen on one arm, Margo on the
other.

35

When someone we love dies, we have a hard time picturing that
person. Even when our child goes away to college, or our wife
or husband just goes to the grocery store, we can't call up a clear
image of our loved one's face. This has happened to me, and I
used to feel bad about it, as though I'd always been too
self-involved to love deeply enough, to see anyone else clearly

enough. I can't see Elvis very clearly. But we're too hard on
ourselves if we think this way. The truth is that we've seen
that loved person so many different times, over so many years,
in so many different moods and lights, in black sorrow and in
bright joy, that there is no one face for us to see.

Even now, though I've seen her almost every day for two
years, though I'll see her again tomorrow, I can't quite
construct Ellen's face behind my eyes.

That night I had Ellen on one arm and Margo on the other.
And though I can't remember Ellen's face, to this day I can
see Margo very clearly, that desperate, wild-eyed white face
floating beside me as we followed Vic and McLaren to the
bar.

36

When I went down to Rogas' desk tonight to light my candle, I
heard a fuss out at the front gate, put on my coat, and walked
outside. It turned out that a carload of kids had driven over
from Queens to see Vic, wanted to get inside the building and
drink with him and listen to some songs on the state-of-the-art
stuff up in the music rooms. They'd read the *Playboy* piece,
"The Class of 1957, Vic Holyfield Style." Vic's men were a little
rough on the kids, I thought, and called Suffolk County cops
to escort these representatives of the Class of 1990 (or whenever)
out of town. . . .

I turned on the pool's underwater lights and took a swim, not
counting laps as I usually do, but just swimming until I felt

like rolling over in the shallow end and quitting. I'm back at
my desk again, but don't feel like writing much, and wonder
what to do with the long night. Maybe I'll skip out and surprise
Ellen with a visit. But I wouldn't want Vic to need somebody
to talk to and light up the red light and then come looking for
me. It's not that he'd make anything out of it if I weren't
here. It's just that I'd feel I let him down. I may be his only
constant right now. He's spent a lot of time in the Ballad
Room lately, all those songs of all those lonely and broken-
hearted people.

Ellen said that Vic still gets many letters from those who
were with us last year. (I don't have to mention that he gets
letters from tens of thousands of others around the country who
want to come here for a year, who are willing to pay to do so.
They think of this place as sort of a *Love Boat* in drydock.) Most
of our friends want Vic to do it again. I'm sure that Vic has
thought about it. I just have the feeling that it shouldn't be
before ten years or so. Maybe not before the year 2000, when
we're all sixty or so. Maybe we'll all be huddled here as the last
seconds of 1999 tick away, maybe taking the world with them,
as some have predicted.

I have a master key and wandered around for a while just
now, looking into some of the bedrooms. In almost every
room a little something has been left behind, maybe wishful
thinking about coming back, maybe something to focus revery
on when away. Joanne Brighton left behind her inscribed copy
of a book of photographs edited by Jacqueline Kennedy
Onassis. Rudy Gasparik's cassette player is in his room. When
I pushed the "on" button, Johnnie and Joe sang "Over the
Mountain, Across the Sea." Clara Edgar's bed is still covered
with a pink bedspread, and there's a teddy bear on her pillow.
Jerry Mortensen's well-underlined volumes of *Harvard Classics*
are still on his bookshelves. Werner and Barbara have left
their pajamas laid out on their beds. Ralph and Edie Thompson
left their grand piano in their room, though we were willing
to ship it home for them, of course. McLaren left his lamppost

drunk, and a full bottle of Jack Daniels on his dresser. Freddie
Elbert, our class queen (who, I'm glad to say, apparently got
Mario Angelo out of the closet last year), left behind his silvery
cock sculpture back scratcher or dildo or whatever it is. I can't
even remember whose room it is where there's an open diary
on the desk with just this written on the first page: "Dear diary,
it's September 199-, and Vic has brought us all back to school
for a second time." Dave Wicks left a basketball on his bed. But
there's not a trace of a reminder in Margo's room, not a book
or a bedspread or a photograph. It looks as if she was never
here. Gary Rizzo left a photograph of his Theresa and his
son. . . .

On my way over here tonight, I walked by Nick's, which is of
course closed, only a night light on over the mirror behind the
counter. . . .

37

There are two hundred billion stars in our Milky Way, our
earth's galaxy. Our earth is a tiny particle in the Milky Way. If
you were to count these stars one a second for twenty-four hours
a day you'd be counting for six thousand years before you had
them all counted. And there are millions of galaxies, maybe
infinite numbers of galaxies. I don't know how long it takes
for light to travel from one side of our Milky Way to the other.
It takes a long, long time.

We forget that we live on a star. We're part of the great
chain of buying and spending. We accumulate. We dole out

our dough for shit we don't need. But maybe the old songs, somehow, connect us with the cosmos again. Maybe they are simple cries of the heart from when we were wide-open and out there taking chances. Our chests were filled with galaxies, so deep were our emotions as our bodies pumped hormones faster than we could adjust to our changing shapes in the mirror. Comets traveled our bloodstreams as we walked the halls of our schools to a rock tempo, or hummed a slow song that seemed to be beating in our chests. The doo-wah and falsetto, the songs of aching love and car wrecks and white sports coats and pink carnations and soldier boys gone away and stories untold and roses and Baby Ruths and sweet sixteens hit by trains and sitting in the balcony—these were not songs to think about. Maybe it's true, as someone said, that the music of my generation was a "plaintive wail," but our songs recorded for us, day by day, who we were. We didn't have to be told that "Donna" was the real name of Richie Valens' girlfriend, and it was a true story of losing her that he sang. How could it have been any other way? We'd hear a song over the radio for the first time, and it would make us shiver even before we heard any of its words.

In music, maybe, the young are always right. They are the ones who tell the truth. Depending on how sophisticated or "educated" we become later on, we're embarrassed by those moving reminders of what in truth we once were, and deny our songs. Vic had risked nothing less than absolute humiliation in the world's eyes. But he knew what we were feeling. A lesser man with Vic's money might have brought us back to listen to classical music in the three rooms upstairs, might have turned the gym into an art gallery, might have tried to impress us with the outer man he'd become. And we'd have gone along with it. And then we'd have gone home after ten months and heard one of the old songs and been split and swept back to truer selves still aching to surface.

We make fun of ourselves, our attachments, but just before we fall asleep at night, should we think of those days, that

music from when we were young, we know again that we once
lived on a star. "Why Don't You Write Me?" we ask our
memories. We go on with our lives, but we keep seeing
ourselves as we were when we spawned rhythms of Milky
Ways beneath our breastbones. "Why Do Fools Fall in Love?"
Never mind. We do. May we never live to be so old that we
don't. We gave ourselves to our music. It now keeps drawing us
back to it. We resist because we're told to. Vic let go. The
writers who understand him understand this, whatever the
music of their own generation is, whatever their educations.
I've been thinking about these things. I happen to think that
there are even lessons here for some of our politicians who
need to understand the people.

Vic said, as I mentioned, that he first heard "Earth Angel"
when Eddie Williams sang it while dribbling a basketball up
the court. I went down to the gym tonight, played that record
about ten times, and dribbled up and down the court, running
with Eddie's voice all the way to Virgo in the dark. For one
moment, I thought I sensed someone on the balcony, watching
me. I shot two hundred billion foul shots with my eyes closed,
and for all I know every one of them went in.

38

First of March. Glittery and cold.

Two nights ago I was here at my desk when I felt the
building shudder slightly. Vic's helicopter was landing. A few
minutes later he and Margo came clattering down the stairs.

I hadn't seen her since last June. Jesus, she *is* stunning, I thought.

She seemed to go out of her way to be friendly. I didn't expect it. She hugged me. I bent over her, lifted her up. Vic had a silly-ass plastered look on his face.

"Come on," Vic said, "we're meeting Ellen."

I didn't even ask where. For all I knew, we'd be flying to Acapulco.

The three of us walked outside to Vic's waiting limo, which took us all of the two blocks to Nick's.

Nick's was candlelit. Ellen was already there. To see that we wouldn't be bothered, two of Vic's men waited in the limo just outside the entrance.

The four of us, alone in the place, punched up some songs and sat at one of the old booths. Vic insisted on making us some BLT's. Margo and Ellen made milk shakes. I crooned along with songs in my best late great Johnny Ace and Jimmy Bowen voices. When I boomed out "I'm stuck witchoo baby," even Margo laughed.

Working over the grill, Vic half shouted, "Margo and I were in Boston tonight, having a drink with the Bird man after the Celts game, talking about you two. All of a sudden we missed you *too* much, you know, and got the hell back here."

We sat down with the food. "Best BLT I've ever had." Margo winked at Ellen and me as she tried to hold her sandwich together. Then she made one of Joan Rivers' gag gestures and fumbled her BLT apart on purpose. This was Margo doing this!

I reached across the table to hold Margo's hands.

"Where you been, stranger?" I asked.

Within a second or two, Margo's eyes filled with tears. She let go of my hands to reach for a tissue.

"That's what we wanted to tell you," Vic said. "That, and something else."

He looked at Margo. At that moment, Cereno and the Bow Ties were singing "Rosemarie."

"Go ahead, Vic," she said. "I'm cool."

"Margo's been in the hospital again. I mean she's been back. She had an operation. We wanted to tell you."

I looked through the front door. I could see the limo's exhaust puffing up through the red taillights. Joe Therrien, Jr., and the Rockets were singing "Roses Are Blooming, Come Back to Me Darling." I felt dizzy, as though my strawberry milk shake had been spiked. I felt as though I were back in a time I thought I'd left behind. I'd seen too much, and now just this news of a friend's illness came close to knocking me off-kilter.

"Margo's been sick. She's been sick since just before we came back to school. She didn't want to tell me. She didn't want us to know. She told me, at last, thank God." Vic had felt himself saying what he said, and was shaken.

He kissed Margo, stroked her hair as though he were comforting a child. She wilted against him.

The room was quiet, the record was changing when she straightened up and said, "I've had a mastectomy." The four of us were holding hands across the table. "I've gotten through it. It was hard on me, harder than I should have allowed it to be. I couldn't help it at the time. I forgive myself, though.... Goddamnit...." She wept, but gritted her teeth and caught her breath again.

"She didn't want to put a damper on anybody's year here," Vic said. "She'd been thinking about telling me, just me, and then Pete died. She thought it would be too much for us to know that she had cancer, you know. And shit, who wants to walk around thinking that all anybody else is thinking about when they see you is whether or not you're going to be under the knife and maybe wearing a false breast before long?" Vic was watching me closely. He knew what I'd been through.

"Listen," Margo said, "I did hope I could get by with radiation and chemotherapy, or, at the most, with removal of some tissue, but I did have to ... I *am* wearing a falsie." She was half laughing and half crying. "But I'm not going to tell you which one. Only my doctor and Vic and I know for sure."

"There's no sign of cancer anywhere else," Vic said. But Margo broke in: "There's a slight shadow on my left lung—it could be something or could be nothing. It's probably nothing. More tests. And Vic's doctors are standing in line to see me. I think he's cleared out a whole floor at the Mayo for me!"

"Margo's going to live to be a hundred," Vic said. "Someday she'll have to sit in the auditorium all by herself and look up into the heavens at the faces of all her deceased classmates."

We were all looking down at the table. It was no time to say anything. I felt that I'd be okay, that I'd made it out again.

"Can I watch them on television in the bar, instead?" Margo asked. "I'll have to if I'm going to have to see your mug when I'm a hundred."

"I told her," Vic said, "that when she thinks of me when I'm gone, I want her to play Screaming Jay Hawkins' "I've Got a Spell on You.' "

The two of them kept slapsticking. Ellen hadn't said a word yet, but broke in on them. "Margo, I'm so glad you told us, I'm so glad." She almost knocked over her milk shake as she pulled Margo's hand to her cheek. "I've always wanted you to be my friend, for us to be real friends. Even in school, Margo." Ellen was crying now. "You're going to be fine, Margo. You have all of us now, and we have you. And the four of us, only the four of us, are not going to keep any more secrets from one another, no matter what. And that's an order! Vic, we're going to make up a contract on this. And Margo is going to sign it this time even if we have to break her fucking arms!"

Vic began to talk. Lower than the Fleetwoods doing "Mr. Blue," he talked, as though he were the only one listening. We all tried to hear him, at first. He moved his head back and forth, mumbling. We let him go for the length of the song. I don't know what he said. He seemed to snap back to himself, and us, between records. I'd never seen him act that way, and haven't again since then.

Both women looked like hell, mascara running down their cheeks. The Platters were finishing "My Prayer." Vic pulled

off his tie and threw it on the floor, rolled up his sleeves, went
to the jukebox. I jumped over the counter and slapped
together inedible sundaes while the three of them made believe
they were Bo Diddley, weaving within the colors of the old
Seaburg, playing invisible guitars, going to London for a
diamond ring, or whatever the fuck it is that Bo goes and
does.

I hit Margo with a whipped cream pie right in the puss. She
drenched me with a milk shake and the four of us slid around
in the mess. Margo held her hand in the air and turned around
under it, stomping her boots to "The Bristol Stomp." We
hollered and whistled.

One of Vic's men peered in on us through the front door,
then saw that we weren't being slaughtered by terrorists, so
disappeared again. Above the Beach Boys, Vic began shouting as
we were dancing. "And we're getting *married,*" he yelled.
"We're getting *married.*" Margo was twirling around, and during
one twirl put the biggest goddamned rock on her ring finger
that I'd ever seen. "Woowee," Ellen screamed. Margo twirled
around under her diamond as big as the Ritz.

We came back here, went up to the Ballad Room, pushed two
couches to face each other. Ellen lit a candle and put it on the
floor between the couches, then turned off the rest of the lights.
Vic lay down with Margo, and Ellen and I lay down together
and faced our two friends as the songs said all the things we
had just begun to say to one another.

39

Vic and Margo have been away for a couple of weeks, settling things, but they call and talk to Ellen every day, and I've heard from them here a couple of times at night. They haven't set a definite date yet, but the wedding, I'm sure, is going to be here at the school. Ellen's pretty sure they want a bash, not just a justice-of-the-peace thing with only a witness or two. I can see it now: Margo's train will reach from the auditorium stage down the stairs all the way out to the front gate, maybe all the way to Nick's.

I've never felt better. I've been shooting baskets for about an hour every night, and then going for a swim, then wandering the building or just sitting here at the desk. I haven't written anything for a couple weeks, but I've slowly gotten back into reading. I found a poetry anthology in a carton of new books that Gillman had never opened. Thirty or so poets about my age, and each has written a prose piece as preface to five or ten poems. Some of the stuff is absolutely unintelligible, as though it were meant to be, as though the poets lived in a world where there are no bricks or helicopters, no mud or trees, no rock songs, no people at work, no sentences that had to make sense. But some of the poems do set off thoughts and feelings inside me. Something in me usually wants to dismiss them, but some of them can't be shrugged away as just screwing around with words.

I found a poem called "Mantle." It's not about a coat or a

fireplace mantel, but about the Mick himself. Its left margin
starts out at the pitcher's mound and bends in across the plate.

MANTLE

Mantle ran so hard, they said,
he tore his legs to pieces.
What is this but spirit?

52 homers in '56, the triple crown.
I was a high school junior, batting
fourth behind him in a dream.

I prayed for him to quit, before
his lifetime dropped below .300.
But he didn't, and it did.

He makes Brylcreem commercials now,
models with open mouths draped around him
as they never were in Commerce, Oklahoma,

where the sandy-haired, wide-shouldered boy
stood up against his barn,
lefty for an hour (Ruth, Gehrig),

then righty (DiMaggio),
as his father winged them in,
and the future blew toward him,

now a fastball, now a slow
curve hanging
like a model's smile.

I'm not sure how much is going on in that first stanza, but it
gives us a ballplayer who kept hurting himself because of his
desire, or spirit, which was too great for his body. Mantle kept
getting hurt, god knows, ripped himself up just by running out

a drag bunt. On top of that, he had a bone disease. He broke
my heart when I was a kid. Then he kept playing, and kept
playing, when he should have retired, until his lifetime batting
average ended up being less than that magic .300.

In his preface the poet says "Mantle" is a love poem. I
suppose it is. But there's a lot of hurt and sorrow there. I've
never seen the hair tonic commercial he mentions, but I've seen
Mantle and Willie Mays in a Blue Bonnet margarine
commercial. They're sitting in high chairs, wearing frilly
bonnets, acting like babies, saying they want margarine,
whining. I was embarrassed for them. Seeing them demean
themselves that way, great athletes that they were, Hall of
Famers—it was pitiful. Thank god that at least Elvis never fell
for any of that, though I remember pitches to him to endorse
boots, after-shave lotion, Cadillacs, western clothes, even a line
of panty hose. He could have saved the companies of some
"friends" with those kinds of endorsements, and he was loyal,
but had the integrity to say no.

There's a lot of sex in the poem, too. The grammar makes for
a blowjob (I almost used the word "fellatio") in the eleventh
line—at least that's the way I hear it—and the ending floats the
model's mouth around the Mick again. So Mickey, from
Commerce, Oklahoma, was destined somehow for the big city.
The poem sees into his future even while he's home with his
father pitching to him, but there's more to the sense of time in
the poem than I can say here. It's almost spooky. And I like
the farmboy's dreams, as he's batting, of the Yankee immortals.
The poem has one thing wrong, though. It leaves something
out. Mickey's uncle, too, used to pitch to him, and he threw
with the opposite hand from Mickey's father, and this turned
the kid into a switch-hitter, in fact.

One day last spring Mickey, Billy Martin, and Whitey Ford
all showed up here at the school at the same time. It turned
out that Vic had known them for years, had partied with them,
had busted up at least one bar with them. Yogi would have
been here, too, but probably headed for Jonestown by mistake,

Vic said. Vic's Stengelese was pretty good: "That fella there, number eight, that fella there is where he is, and that's somewhere, when he's there behind the plate, and when he isn't, then he digs in for the next time, that fella there."

We'd thought of having a baseball tournament similar to the basketball one, maybe get Bobby Wine and Yaz and some of the old Yankees and Giants and Boys of Summer together, but Vic's interest and mine fell away from that. I guess a lot of it had to do with Pete's death. We'd have done it for him so that he could have pitched against his old heroes.

But we did get together for softball games last spring, and it was on an afternoon in April that I found myself pitching to Mickey, who appeared from nowhere, another of Vic's surprises. This character in Yankee pinstripes—I couldn't tell who in hell it was—came dragging a big bat up to the left side of the plate. At first I actually thought it was McLaren, who is a wide-shouldered and sandy-haired son of a bitch, but then I knew. Mickey smiled—he had some hard miles on him, and Jerry Lee flashed into my mind, but he still looked boyish—and pointed his bat over toward the school about six hundred feet away in right field.

I made a show of conferring with Vic, and then brushed Mickey back twice, looping slow pitches behind his head. One hit his bat as he was ducking forward out of the way. He made a mock charge to the mound. Vic from first base and my other infielders and I surrounded him and hoisted him up. Mickey Mantle. Do you remember those white dotted lines in photographs in *The Daily News* that traced the trajectories of balls he hit? One almost went out of the Stadium over the right-field stands. I never got to the Stadium when I was a kid. It was too much of a hassle to drive there, but my father took me to Ebbets Field in Brooklyn a few times. My father loved those Bums. If he were still alive, I'd have him here at the school and would have Duke Snyder and Roy Furillo, his favorites, here for him. I'd buy up enough of Brooklyn to put

up Ebbets Field again and bring the Bums back. I swear I
would....

Mickey Mantle. What didn't I think about as we set him back
down in the batter's box?

Vic slipped me a different ball to pitch to number seven.

I gave him the fattest pitch I could. Mickey got under it, got
his wrists through it, lofted it as though it were a golf ball. He
sailed it way over Werner's and Barbara's heads in right field.
Don Pike ran right out from under his wig going after it. The
ball must have been made of silly putty, or whatever that stuff is
that bounces like crazy. It took one or two tremendous
bounces and hit the school. (Funniest damned thing, and I don't
know why I even mention it here, but someone was standing
over by the school, watching us, seeming awfully forlorn,
someone whose silvery shirt glistened like a cocoon in the
school's shade. I can still see that person, and now I realize that
it must have been Phil!) Anyway, Mick rounded the bases in
his heavy-shouldered way. I threw my cap on the ground and
stomped on it. Eddie Rogas, believe it or not, actually busted
his gut yelling for a relay throw so that we could try to throw
the Mick out. He yelled at Werner and Barbara.

Mick got on his knees in front of the plate and tagged home
by kissing it.

That night we staged a mock fight in the bar, destroyed the
place pretty good. Billy Martin said it was the first time he'd
been paid to raise hell. He asked Vic's man to stand aside, and
threw a bar-stool strike to the nude painted on the mirror.

40

First time I've been out of town since that trip with Vic to Atlantic City. I flew from MacArthur to D.C. and stood by the Viet Nam memorial for a day, then flew back home. I haven't said a single thing about all that, and won't. I haven't said a single *direct* word. But that's not arthritis in my shoulder.

I feel only notations in me tonight.

I've been reading more these days—to pass the time, but also because I've been opening up to it, and *making* time by reading, as Vic once said Emerson said. On the side, I've even written a few poems, but you won't have to worry about suffering through any of them.

I remember that Margie Eaton's parrot got out of its cage once last year. Its squawking threw me, reminded me of things I'd heard. It flew into the gym, where it stayed for a couple days until it got hungry and Margie was able to entice it back down into its cage.

Mr. Till asked me if I've lost my credit card. He meant I hadn't been using it at all. I've had no need for it. I don't need anything. I still have most of that stash of cash I won on my birthday, in fact. I still don't even have a thousand miles on my Buick.

April 10th already. The wedding is to be in mid-June. The place will be packed. Not only all our friends who spent the year here will be back, but friends from Vic's other life will be here, as well as Margo's family and friends. *People* already says

that it's going to be the hottest ticket in history. It's nice to be
on the inside around here. I feel at home. "All the cats wanna
dance with/sweet little sixteen."

The lilac and honeysuckle are budding again out in front of
the building. I'll blink my eyes and they'll be budding again
next year.

A few nights ago, for the first time, I began to tell Ellen some
things about Elvis, his karate period when I spent the most
time with him, when he'd let me talk to him, when he seemed
to listen and seemed to want to know what had happened to me.
There were weeks when I spent more time with him than
anybody else did. Talking to Ellen, I felt myself coming out
from under swamp water in a way I can't describe. I'd put so
much out of my mind, but must have put it somewhere, and it
bothered me from wherever that was, worried me like a wasp,
was never truly off my mind. Tonight, the candle down at
Rogas' desk is clear and bright, seems to be only a few feet
away. I feel on top of things, centered, relieved, balanced. I
could snuff the candle with a BB gun hip shot tonight. Tonight,
I can see with my whole body, which is just what Sadaharu
Oh's coach on the Tokyo Giants told him he had to do. Oh was
told that he had a blind hip, that he had to learn to see with
his hip when he hit. I love that idea, and understand it. Karate,
too, is the art of seeing.

Yesterday, Ratch Casano blasted in on his low-slung cycle,
shook all the sparrows out of the ivy in front of the building. I
talked with him for only a few minutes. He's been on the road,
but had heard something about Vic's wedding. I told him
Saturday, June 12th. "Hey, Ratch," I said, "no Hell's Angels,
eh?" Ratch has the damnedest friends. "June twelfth, June
twelfth," he said, and roared off again for another reunion with
a buddy somewhere. He'll be back, I know.

Ellen and I got a card announcing the marriage of Katie Kirk
and Louis Soskin.

I've found out some things about Margo's missing years, but
that's a whole other story, and Margo and Vic are the ones to

tell it, if anybody. I've only wanted to tell you about the year of
the return, though I've gotten off the track sometimes, I
know.

Lars Svanberg is supposed to show up in about an hour. We'll
shoot some baskets and go for a swim. Then I'll take him
around the school, as I've showed other classmates around when
they've dropped in. They want to see the place again. They
know I'm here during the nights, and this is when they show
up. They wonder if they were ever here, and need to walk
around the building and reassure themselves that they hadn't
dreamed the whole thing. Louise Axel stopped in a couple
weeks ago. I thought it would be a sad visit, but it wasn't. I told
her that Vic had made sure that her and Pete's room would
always be left just as it was. This seemed to me a little
morbid—I've never been back to Graceland—but Vic had
anticipated Louise's reaction better than I had. She said she
wished Vic were there so that she could hug him. She'd see
him at the wedding, of course, she said. She hung some of Pete's
clothes in the closet in their room, including his letter sweater
from the old days. He still had his fucking letter sweater. Pete, I
miss you. . . .

So far as I know, Margo is okay. She and Vic always tell
Ellen where they can be reached when they're out of town, as
they usually are these days. A few weeks ago, at about three in
the morning, one of Vic's men came in from the front gate
with an express delivery for me: they'd sent me, from Vic's pad
in Waikiki, an aquarium with a beautiful pair of kissing
gouramis in it.

I don't have to be here at all, of course.

I have a picture in my mind of passing the chapel one
evening in January or February the year we lived here, and
seeing Margo and Vic there by themselves. I don't know why I
remember this now. Wedding associations, I guess. Margo
must have been so miserable at that time. How could she have
kept so much from Vic for so long?

Eddie Williams lives! He was in South America, doing who

knows what. Apparently, he was in Nam, too. Ellen says he'll
be at the wedding. I've got to be there when Vic sees Eddie
again for the first time.

Ellen and I are going to be married, too, but not until late in
the summer, and then very quietly. We'll ask Margo and Vic
to be our witnesses, find a pastor in a small town somewhere—
maybe Charlie Edmunds, come to think of it—and try to
make a marriage that lasts all the way. What the hell good is
anything if you can't begin storing up memories *with* someone
you love? We both feel this way. She's convinced now, too, that
I'll be okay. She wasn't, I think, as long as I was so paranoid
about certain things. She told me one thing that surprised me.
She said that when we first met again she was a little afraid of
me. I told her I felt more like a dishrag than a danger to
anybody. Now, she's not worried. A couple days ago she asked
me, in fact, how, after what I've been through, I could still be so
sentimental. I know what she means, and don't know the
answer. She's glad I am, she says.

After high school Ellen worked as a secretary in New York
for several years, and bumped into Vic by accident sometime
after he'd finished at Cornell. A few years after that, needing
someone he could trust, he called her, flew her to Texas, and
she became his right-hand woman. She knows him, I'm sure,
better than anybody else does. She says he did speak of me
often all those years, spoke of getting his old basketball team
together. Vic had seen the Robert Mitchum movie about a
Pennsylvania basketball team's reunion, and this had gotten him
to thinking, but it probably wasn't until Margo's telegram that
he himself knew just what it was that he'd been thinking about,
or half knew.

Vic told me he once saw Elvis in Las Vegas. He hated what
he saw, and maybe seeing Elvis made him repress memories of
high school. Vic went about his business, filling his haymow
with gold. Elvis went about his business, killing himself,
becoming more and more the buffoon and fiend, and no one
could pray or club or kick him off that course. I dislocated his

jaw once, in fact—it was on purpose, after a wounding thing he'd said to someone else, but he didn't know it had been on purpose. I slapped it back in for him, and it swelled up real good and he couldn't talk for a couple days.

For a few years when I was a kid, when I didn't want to be a Yankee to take over for Mickey when his playing days were over, I was thinking of being a nurseryman. I used to plant flowers, loved marigolds, nasturtiums, petunias, the coleuses and cacti that I kept inside all winter. Once, in a field in Nesconset, I found about a hundred mimosa seedlings, transplanted them to our garden, thought of selling them when they got bigger, buying an acre of land for my nursery from the profits. But I didn't know I had to cover them up for the winter, and they died. My favorite Island tree, though, is the dogwood. I've had talks with old Tony. He's going to put in a few dogwood trees inside the fence out in front this month. I've asked him, maybe, to alternate white and pink ones.... Maybe, one of these years, I'll buy a nursery and get my back into some good work.

Doc Saunders isn't feeling well these days, I hear. He's back in Dallas. Ellen talks with him once in a while. He tells her he had a hell of a lot of fun here. Gruff as he is, he always reminds me of old "Doc" in *Gunsmoke,* and I know he has the same kind of soul. He had a lot more to do last year than I've reported here, everything from allergy tests to insulin injections to setting Gil L'Hommidieu's broken collarbone.

Vic didn't have a good home situation when he was young. Before he went off to Oberlin, he told me, he taped all his old rock and roll records. He couldn't carry all those records with him, and he wasn't sure his mother wouldn't throw them all out on him when he was away—maybe, in fact, she'd blamed his sickness that summer on that music. Anyway, those must be the tapes he gave me. I'll save them. In some spots on them—as in The Platters' "Only You," he said—he can hear his seventeen-year-old self singing quietly along, or whistling. He didn't know he was picking himself up. "He won't let me

listen to those tapes," Margo said as Vic blushed. "Margo, I have
them in a vault in Switzerland," Vic said, winking at me. But
maybe he does, the originals.

Vic had been an excellent student in high school, made a 90+
average without any apparent strain. His basketball and
baseball teammates didn't pay any attention to that, didn't hold
that against him. He even played the lead in a couple plays. I
never went to a play. I was always reading one book or another,
but not one that had anything to do with classes at the time,
and I was in the bottom half of my class. Oberlin, apparently, is
a fine-arts school filled with art-brat types. Vic was miserable,
had maybe misjudged himself. Also, he says, he thinks
something chemical happened to him during a year or two
back then. He lost something he once had, was unable, for
example, to respond to literature, couldn't act, didn't enjoy
concerts he was attending or even a girlfriend's piano playing.
Wandering around the Oberlin campus one night, by accident
or some strange fate, he said, he found himself in an advanced
calculus classroom, everything clicking together for him, as
though he'd always known what the professor was saying and
calculating on the board, as though he knew what the
professor would say and write next, and knew what came after
that. Vic cannot even begin to talk to me about such things. I
don't want to understand, even if I could. It was painful to
watch Mr. Flamenbaum, our old algebra teacher, talk math to
Vic during our year back and then try to follow when Vic got
excited and started putting equations on the board—but I've
always believed in genius, and know that something of the
miraculous must have happened to Vic. I don't have to know
the nuts and bolts of it. I don't know what it is, either, but I
have something inside me, too, that nobody else has, unformed
as it is right now.

When I went to college, it was for physical education. After
three years, fucked up, I drifted down south. Two years in
Nam. Enough said. I don't have a degree. I've gotten by. My
brain has gotten back to where it was, I think. It scares me to

think that I may have done irreparable damage to myself.
Sometimes, maybe, I don't think as clearly as I used to. But
I'm not sure. It could be that I don't want to think, at least not
in a western way. I believe in cultivating the kind of wise
thoughtlessness that Zen poets talk about. It's a kind of quiet
knowing. But, in any case, drugs didn't do me any good.
Unless they did, blanking out other things. But something in me
saved me. I've no other explanation. The "it." I surfaced by
myself, and maybe by something I found at the center of my
discipline. Elvis never did find that center. I could have
broken his fucking jaw three times and it wouldn't have
mattered. He was mainlining when I left.

Vic has been leaving batches of photographs from last year on
my desk. I stare at each one for a long time, trying to see what
else there is in the photo that Vic wasn't aiming for. There's one
photo I keep coming back to. It's from last spring, when Vic
took the Class of 1957 to the White House for a reception.
Margo must have taken the photo. It's a simple shot of Vic
standing with the President, but Vic is so obviously *not there* in
the Oval Office even while he's there. He's looking, it seems to
me, right at Margo as she takes the picture. It's eerie. I've never
seen a photograph before in which there is so much tension
between the subject (or in this case one of the subjects) and the
photographer. The lame-duck President is smiling and so
relaxed that it's as though he's just won another congressional
battle for more missiles, but Vic is riveted to the eyes behind
the camera. His own eyes seem hollow, as in some statues I've
seen. This may, of course, all be my imagination and a trick
of the Oval Office light, but I know Margo did meet Vic at the
White House, even if she didn't fly in to Washington with the
class. I flew in to Washington with Vic in his helicopter but
didn't go with him to the White House. He knew where I
would be. I met him that evening at the Press Club for dinner,
and then the two of us flew back to Smithtown, each of us
silent all the way. That was one night we were both glad to see
the searchlights of the school roof come into view at last over

the Island, to land quickly, descend into the dark school, and to
leave each other alone. Yes, Margo must have taken that
picture. He only had eyes for her. . . .

I want to go on with these notes, but I hear Lars coming in. I
just spooked myself. I'll be glad to play some ball.

41

I was at my desk the other night and could hear the Flamingoes
singing "I Only Have Eyes for You," then The Danleers doing
"One Summer Night," even The Elegants singing "Little Star."
I figured Vic had moved over to the Fast Dance Room, and
went upstairs to see my main man.

I wondered if Margo would be with him. I hadn't heard or
felt the copter land, but sometimes wind or rain softened the
landings. Sometimes I drifted away at my desk into this journal
or into a poem.

The third-floor hall was lit with only a few blue night lamps.
Then it happened. When I passed Elvis's room, I thought I
saw someone. To tell the truth, I thought for just a moment
that I saw Elvis, a hard and lean Elvis sitting in a chair. But
then the light in which he appeared went black, blacker than his
hair. He seemed to implode. I didn't go in.

There were low lights on in the Ballad Room, but no music,
no Vic, no Margo, no one. It was so quiet that I sat at one of
the easy-chair consoles, put on earphones, and played some songs
I hadn't heard in a long time. That settled me. I'm still okay. I
don't expect it to happen again. The apparition must have been

some kind of brain glitch, a sniglet of the neurons, a shooting
star, incoming. Still, and I won't mention this again but will say
it once and for all, I can't tell you how much I miss that man.
I still feel as though I abandoned him. I shouldn't feel this way.
Maybe some anger going the other way would help. He knew
what I'd been through, but didn't live so that he would always
be there for me. He abandoned me, abandoned all of us. He
deserted. But I've dreamed of him following me in one of his
Cadillacs, yelling "Billy, Billy" to me, trying to get me back to
Memphis.

One of the poets used the phrase "irreversible loss." I know
what that means. Sometimes still my chest seems to empty out,
but then I think of Ellen and I'm okay again.... I bet you
never heard a song by The Diablos called "The Way You Dog
Me Around." Not the words so much, but its sounds are the
equivalent of the emotions I'm talking about. But you can
name your own song. Irreversible. Final.

I never get tired of walking these halls, standing in one spot
and then another, closing my eyes, holding out my arms,
throwing a fake or a kick at a shadow, whirling into and out of
a blue light, standing in one spot and then another in complete
stillness for minutes at a time. Sometimes I'll play a record in
one of the rooms and take a three-minute walk, listening to it
diminish, then come back to it just as it ends. If it's a fast dance,
I move quickly, of course, sometimes along a couple of floors.
If it's a slow one, sometimes I'll only amble and sway for fifty
feet down the hall before coming back to choose another song.
Did you ever hear Jack Scott's "Indiana Waltz"? I'd be
embarrassed if anybody saw me still doing the four-point
waltz Coach Mularz forced me to learn in gym class in high
school, but you've got your own secret moments. But maybe
my friends can see me now. Maybe they feel me thinking about
them right now and are putting records on and making some
private moves. Maybe they'll get up, right now, between
paragraphs, to dance to an oldie, even something as sweet and

corny as "Let's Go Steady" or "Sitting in the Balcony," maybe to
Jack's "Midgie" or "The Indiana Waltz" itself.

Sometimes I make believe that one of the groups is in the
building again, maybe The Shirelles doing "Baby, It's You," and
I dance away from them or toward them along the halls
during the song. You haven't heard anything if you haven't
heard "Will You Still Love Me Tomorrow" the length of an
empty hall at night in your old high school. The echoes contain
the whole world.

I'm still surprising myself with how easily I've been writing
along here lately. Let it be.

I don't usually have any music on here at my desk. I want to
hear what's going on in the building, just in case. But I get up
often, and if I don't go upstairs for a song or two, I'll just
whistle or hum as I walk and stretch, finding my way to my
candle. I can see its light even when my eyes are closed. I
haven't killed myself yet.

I'm okay when I sit in Elvis's room or listen to him. But I
can't bring myself to read any recent book on him, the
Goldman book, for example. The truth hurts, and Goldman
probably tells the truth, but there are things in our lives more
important than the truth. You and I, during our best moments,
know this. I can make a candle appear in the dark in my
room, now, and can make it disappear. So to speak.

Elvis once said to me ... Never mind. I still have to keep
him mostly to myself. As you do.

42

Dug out a book on the history of rock and roll. My favorite chapter, it turns out—I skipped the one on Elvis—is on Phil. The author, Nik Cohn, goes over Phil's whole weird career but ends up talking about how, in the end, there has never been any lasting fulfillment, nothing to build on in any meaningful way. Phil may be lost, the author implies, but in spite of that, and I want to quote, "He still stands as the definitive rock 'n roll saga. No one else had so perfectly caught its potentials, and also its limitations. He's been everything that pop did best—fast and funny and crazed, full of style and marvelous follies, distinctly heroic; he had shown just how fast the medium went sour. This was a world made for magnificent flashes, combustions that could never sustain. Get into it two-handed. Stampede right through it and then quit dead, without a backward glance. Don't cruise and don't admire the view. Above all, don't ever stop to think."

43

Vic and Margo were blessed with good weather for their
wedding.

They exchanged vows in the chapel, then walked through a
depth of flowers and through their friends lining both sides of
the hall all the way to the auditorium. Vic wore a crimson and
white tux, Margo an off-white gown with a crimson lace belt.
You've seen the picture spreads in the news magazines.

In the auditorium they stood under a starry night sky,
revolving—at the last second a wide-awake Louise rushed up
to get all of Margo's train onto the stage or it would have
wrapped everybody up as the stage turned—laughing, making us
all laugh as Jimmy Clanton came over the speakers singing "A
Million to One," where Jimmy's parents give those odds
against the success of young love. But by the end of the record,
people had stopped giggling, had been sent back into their
time-brains again. Then "There's a Moon Out Tonight" came
on, Vic holding out his arms, singing to Margo, making us
laugh again, down on his knees like Al Jolson as he wondered,
"O Darlin' where have you been?" When "You're Driving Me
Crazy" came on, it was Margo's turn, and she brought down the
house.

Flash bulbs were popping, Vic and Margo were slowly
revolving, songs were coming into and away from us. We
heard "To the Aisle," and I actually *heard* those silly and clever
lyrics for the first time: "You might start with a simple

conversation,/Like 'Darling, won't you put me on trial?' " The
Dubs sang "Could This Be Magic," and then the opening
piano tremble of "Earth Angel" itself began. Vic looked at
Margo steadily during the song, kissed her at the end. I guess
there will never be anything comic about that song for any of
us.

Ray Charles was there and sang "Margo, It's You." This made
Margo cry, and got to Ellen, too.

A chair was brought up on the stage, and Margo sat down.
Vic knelt to remove her garter. He lifted her gown slowly, slid
it slowly up along her thigh. I was close enough to see what
Margo had tucked under her garter. It was a ring, Vic's high
school ring. Margo took the ring from the shocked Vic and put
it on the ring finger of her right hand. Vic almost fainted. . . .
Margo stood up and timed her revolutions perfectly so that you
know, of course, who caught the garter.

These shenanigans went on for about an hour before the
banquet. The banquet was set up in the gym, where a
forty-foot waterfall formed the backdrop. Before too long,
McLaren was sitting in one of the pools beneath it. . . . I guess
that as best man I was supposed to say a few words, but I knew
Vic and Margo would understand if I begged off. I did
manage a simple toast to them. . . . Ellen asked Ratch Casano to
read the congratulatory telegram from President Reagan.
Ratch, in the right spirit, substituted a few words, beginning
with "Dear Fuck," instead of "Dear Vic."

Eddie Williams never did show up, or if he did I never did
see him. I don't like the feeling I have about him. I hope I'm
wrong. I'll look for him when I get a chance.

The waterfall stayed as background for the ball that evening.
Designers had created a wildflower meadow at its base, a
re-creation—except with thousands of real wildflowers—of our
senior prom. Vic and Margo came strolling in, busting through
the red-and-white crepe-paper curtain to "Night Owl." They'd
made up a little four-step. Little yips and hoots accompanied
them. You had to be there.

Bruce Springsteen performed a few numbers live, but even with his feeling for the music of the '50s and '60s, he at first tried out some socially conscious things, and seemed out of place. Maybe this was one day in our lives for pure and simple singing about the joy and silliness and heartbroken loveliness of being alive. He was sensitive enough, after about fifteen minutes, to feel this, and broke out into the sweetest version of "The Story of a Boy and a Girl" I'd heard in thirty years. "He knew someday that she would return," Bruce sang to Margo. I could almost hear something in his voice that could almost make me understand how the young today could call him "The Boss."

Vic and I, Margo and Ellen were sitting together at our table under the balcony when Willie Nelson set up and began his session. We all listened to "To All the Girls We've Loved Before." When Willie began "You Were Always on My Mind," Vic stood up and touched my shoulder and excused the two of us for a while.

We walked upstairs, sipping champagne, chatting with Ted Kennedy and Wolfman Jack and Arnold Palmer and others along the way. Upstairs, Vic unlocked Elvis's room. We slipped in and closed the door before anyone could follow us. Vic locked it from inside. He had me sit beside him in one of the two chairs in front of the alcove, where a small square stage had been set up.

For a few minutes we just sat quietly in the dark room, decompressing. We could hear the party noises as though from far away, years away. The June moonlight filtered in through the maples. I thought we'd just sit there, quietly, not talking, not needing to say anything. It was the Lord who made light, I was thinking, as moonlight came in. *Light* was enough. Anyone lucky enough to be above ground in the light had enough. Anyone lucky enough to be above ground.

Then Elvis was there. I didn't know what had happened. Elvis, the lean, hard Elvis, was there, in three dimensions, in four dimensions, looking at us. He was sitting in a chair, in a shiny black leather jacket with his collar turned up, in black pants and boots, black leather wristband with silver studs, alone in the world, but with us. I was afraid. He was not real, I knew, or thought I knew, but I didn't know what had happened.

But then I did. Vic had made a hologram of Elvis. I'd seen one just once before, a single rose revolving on a pedestal in the Smithsonian. Elvis was here, but he was made only of light. He looked at us with that sullen, curled-lip sneer.

He sang "Playing for Keeps," the words "This time it's real" moving into me with a shudder. Then "It's Now or Never." I sat there in a trance. I could close my eyes and see Elvis as clearly as I did when my eyes were open. Vic leaned over and whispered that there was one more song.

Elvis was singing "If I Can Dream." I stood up, walked onto the stage. I stood as close to him as I could, trying not to block any portion of the light that had to flow into him upward and downward from all angles and directions, but portions of him vanished, no matter which way I moved. I reached my arm into my friend's chest, as though I could touch his heart, but my hand disappeared into blackness.

Elvis disappeared. Vic and I sat in the dark of that room for as long as I can remember.